Sherlock Holmes

A Play in Two Acts

by
Arthur Conan Doyle
and William Gillette

A SAMUEL FRENCH ACTING EDITION

SAMUEL FRENCH

FOUNDED 1830

New York Hollywood London Toronto

SAMUELFRENCH.COM

BROADHURST THEATRE

James Nederlander, Inc.
**The Shubert Organization, Kennedy Center Productions, Inc.
Adela Holzer, Eddie Kulukundis and Victor Lurie**

present

By arrangement with the Governors of the
**ROYAL SHAKESPEARE THEATRE,
STRATFORD-UPON-AVON, ENGLAND**

THE ROYAL SHAKESPEARE COMPANY'S PRODUCTION

JOHN WOOD   PHILIP LOCKE

in

SHERLOCK HOLMES

a play by

ARTHUR CONAN DOYLE and WILLIAM GILLETTE

| DENNIS COONEY | LYNNE LIPTON | RICHARD LUPINO | CHRISTINA PICKLES | RON RANDELL | TONY TANNER |

ARTHUR BURGHARDT   TOBIAS HALLER   MICHAEL HAWKINS
KIM HERBERT   DIANA KIRKWOOD   SUSAN MERRIL-TAYLOR
JOE MUZIKAR   ROBERT PERAULT   ROBERT PHALEN

FRED STUTHMAN   MATTHEW TOBIN
ROCK TOWNSEND   RICHARD WOODS

Music Arranged by   *Lighting Designed by*
MICHAEL LANKESTER   **NEIL PETER JAMPOLIS**

Scenery and Costumes Designed by
CARL TOMS

Directed by
FRANK DUNLOP

ROYAL SHAKESPEARE COMPANY

CHARACTERS
(*In Order of Appearance*)

MADGE LARRABEE .... *Barbara Leigh-Hunt*
JOHN FORMAN .... *Harry Towb*
JAMES LARRABEE .... *Nicholas Selby*
TERESE .... *Pamela Miles*
SIDNEY PRINCE .... *Trevor Peacock*
ALICE FAULKNER .... *Mel Martin*
SHERLOCK HOLMES .... *John Wood*
PROFESSOR MORIARTY .... *Philip Locke*
JOHN .... *Michael Mellinger*
ALFRED BASSICK .... *Martin Milman*
BILLY .... *Sean Clarke*
DOCTOR WATSON .... *Tim Pigott-Smith*
JIM CRAIGIN .... *Morgan Sheppard*
THOMAS LEARY .... *Keith Taylor*
"LIGHTFOOT" McTAGUE .... *Joe Marcell*
PARSONS .... *Arthur Blake*
SIR EDWARD LEIGHTON .... *John Keston*
COUNT VON STALBURG .... *John Bott*
NEWSBOY .... *Robert Cook*
LONDONERS and OTHERS .... *Wendy Bailey,*
Joseph Charles, Alan Coates, Robert Cook,
Joe Marcell, Michael Walker
* *Kim Herbert*
VIOLINIST .... *Christopher Tarle*

* *Replacements*

4

AMERICAN COMPANY

CHARACTERS

(In Order of Appearance)

MADGE LARRABEE .... *Christina Pickles*
JOHN FORMAN .... *Richard Lupino*
JAMES LARRABEE .... *Ron Randell*
TERESE .... *Diana Kirkwood*
                            * *Elizabeth Swain*
SIDNEY PRINCE .... *Tony Tanner*
                            * *Geoff Garland*
ALICE FAULKNER .... *Lynne Lipton*
                            * *Diana Kirkwood*
SHERLOCK HOLMES .... *John Wood*
                            * *Patrick Horgan*
                            * *John Neville*
                            * *Robert Stephens*
PROFESSOR MORIARTY .... *Philip Locke*
                            * *Clive Revill*
                            * *Alan Sues*
JOHN .... *Mathew Tobin*
ALFRED BASSICK .... *Robert Phalen*
BILLY .... *Tobias Haller*
DOCTOR WATSON .... *Dennis Cooney*
JIM CRAIGIN .... *Richard Woods*
THOMAS LEARY .... *Arthur Burghardt*
"LIGHTFOOT" McTAGUE .... *Richard Council*
                            * *Kim Herbert*
PARSONS .... *Mathew Tobin*
SIR EDWARD LEIGHTON .... *Patrick Morgan*
COUNT VON STALBURG .... *Fred Stuthman*
NEWSBOY .... *Rock Townsend*
                            * *Jeffrey Hillock*
LONDONERS and OTHERS ...... *Susan Merril-Taylor,*
            Michael Hawkins, Robert Perault,
            Rock Townsend, Kim Herbert
                            * *Jeffrey Hillock*
VIOLINIST .... *Christopher Tarle*

* *Replacements*

5

ACT ONE

INTERMISSION

ACT TWO

The play is set in London in 1891.

". . . They still live for all that love them well: in a romantic chamber of the heart: in a nostalgic country of the mind where it is always 1895."

VINCENT STARRETT
The Private Life of Sherlock Holmes

SHERLOCK HOLMES

OPENING LINK SCENE

VIOLINIST *resembling famous silhouette of* SHERLOCK
HOLMES *facially on Stage by* S. L. *edge of revolve*
[*mark on floor*]. *Starts to play at end of second
solo phrase of the violin on tape.*

As the Curtain goes up, the NEWSBOY *enters from the
pit* S. R., *stands three feet on Stage from edge of
pit as* TWO POLICEMEN *enter from* D. S. R. *and*
D. S. L. *and walk slowly to center, nod to one another, cross and exit opposite sides.*

NEWSBOY. "Evening News!"—Evening News! Triple
murderer arrested at Paddington! . . . read all about
it. Beer up to two pennies a pint: Cruel blow to the
British working man.

(*As the* NEWSBOY *starts speaking, an* OLD LADY *enters
from the pit* S. L. *with a jug—pitcher—singing
"My Old Man." She puts a coin in the* VIOLINIST'S
*tin cup that hangs on the end of his violin, crosses
the Stage and exits* D. S. R. FORMAN *enters* D. S. R.,
crosses to the VIOLINIST *past the* POLICEMEN *and
puts a note in the* VIOLINIST'S *cup then crosses to
the* NEWSBOY.)

FORMAN. Boy! Boy!
NEWSBOY. Sir?
FORMAN. Is that the latest edition?
NEWSBOY. Yes, sir. Straight from Fleet Street, sir.
(FORMAN *takes a paper, pays for it, crosses above the*
NEWSBOY *and slightly to* S. R.)
FORMAN. Beer up to two pennies a pint! Will things
never stop going up? (FORMAN *exits* D. S. R. *bumping
into the* OLD LADY *who re-enters a little drunk and
weaving with full pitcher from* D. S. R.)

7

NEWSBOY. Evening News! Evening News! (*The* OLD
LADY *snatches a paper from the* NEWSBOY *and crosses*
C. *The* POLICEMAN *re-enters* D. S. L. *and crosses slowly
to* C.) Here . . . that'll cost you a penny to read that,
missus. (NEWSBOY *follows the* OLD LADY S. L.) Old
lady drunk in West Norwood Road . . . Special Edition!

(*The* OLD LADY *turns and hits the* NEWSBOY *with the
newspaper. He falls* C. *The* OLD LADY *is confronted
by the* POLICEMAN *and exits hurriedly* S. L. *pit. The*
NEWSBOY *gets up and exits* S. L. *The* POLICEMAN
waves the VIOLINIST *to move on, then exits* D. S. L.
The VIOLINIST *crosses the Stage and exits* U. S. R.)

ACT ONE

SCENE 1

*The Scene is the drawing room at Edelweiss Lodge,
an old house, situated in a lonely district in a
little-frequented part of London. The furniture is
old and decayed with the exception of the baby
grand piano. The desk is very solid.*

FORMAN *enters the house having just bought a newspaper from the newsboy in the* PROLOGUE.
FORMAN *picks up silver salver from hall table
as he runs in. He moves* C. L. *near the piano and
opens the paper.* MADGE *enters on the balcony,
sees him reading the paper, then closes the door
and comes down the stairs.* FORMAN *folds the
paper and puts it on the salver and holds it out
to her. She takes the paper as she passes him
going* D. S. *and sitting on the ottoman* D. S. L. *side.*

FORMAN. Pardon, ma'am, but one of the maids
wishes to speak to you. (MADGE *reads the paper.*)

MADGE. I can't spare the time now.

FORMAN. Very well, ma'am. (*He starts to leave. She does not look up from the paper.*)

MADGE. Which maid was it?

FORMAN. Terese, ma'am.

MADGE. Terese! (*She stops reading the paper.*)

FORMAN. Yes, ma'am.

MADGE. Have you any idea what she wants?

FORMAN. Not the least, ma'am.

MADGE. She must tell you. I'm very busy, and I can't see her unless I know.

FORMAN. I'll say so, ma'am. (FORMAN *turns and starts to exit* U. L. C. MADGE *looks at the newspaper. Thinking she is alone, she puts the newspaper down on the* S. R. *side of the ottoman, stands, goes to the desk, pushes aside the curtain in front of the safe that is in the center section of the lower half of the desk and kneels in front of the safe checking the dial.* FORMAN *moves* U. R. C. *and* D. S. R. *of the round table observing* MADGE. MADGE *senses that someone is still in the room. She pushes the curtain in front of the safe, stands, turns and sees* FORMAN *who bows to her.*) I could get nothing from her, ma'am. She insists that she must speak to you herself.

MADGE. Tell her to wait till tomorrow. (FORMAN *moves* C. S. *toward* MADGE.)

FORMAN. I asked her to do that, ma'am, and she said she would not be here tomorrow.

MADGE. Judson! (MADGE *moves to* C. S. *above the ottoman toward* FORMAN *and continues to the* D. S. R. *side of the ottoman.*) How did you happen to imagine that I would be interested in this marriage announcement? (MADGE *picks up the newspaper from the* D. S. R. *side of the ottoman.*)

FORMAN. I could 'ardly help it, ma'am.

MADGE. I suppose you have overheard certain references to the matter between myself and my brother?

FORMAN. I 'ave, ma'am, but I would never have

referred to it in the least if I did not think it might be of some importance to you, ma'am.

MADGE. Oh no, of no special importance! We know the parties concerned, and are naturally interested in the event. (MADGE *goes to the round table* S. R. C. *and puts the newspaper down on the* D. S. *end of the table.*) Of course, you do not imagine there is anything more.

FORMAN. Certainly not, ma'am. (MADGE *turns to him as she crosses* S. L. *to the desk.*) Anyway, if I did imagine there was something more, I'm sure you would find it to your interest, ma'am, to remember my faithful services in helpin' to keep it quiet. (MADGE *turns to* FORMAN.)

MADGE. Judson, (MADGE *crosses* C. S. *toward* FORMAN.) what sort of a fool are you? You are a self-confessed forger.

FORMAN. No! Don't speak out like that! It was . . . it was in confidence . . . I told you in confidence, ma'am.

MADGE. Well, I'm telling you in confidence that at the first sign of any underhand conduct on *your* part this little episode of yours will . . .

FORMAN. Yes, yes! I will bear it in mind, ma'am. I will bear it in mind! (MADGE *crosses* S. L. *to the desk.*)

MADGE. Very well! Now, as to the maid, Terese. Why does she think she will not be here tomorrow?

FORMAN. It has occurred to me, ma'am, that she may have taken exceptions to some occurrences which she thinks she 'as seen going on in this 'ouse.

MADGE. I'll raise her wages. If it isn't money that she wants, I'll see her myself.

FORMAN. Very well, ma'am. (FORMAN *bows and exits* U. C. L. MADGE *stands a moment then there is the sound of the front door closing* U. R. JIM LARRABEE *enters carrying a newspaper. He passes* MADGE *as he goes to the desk* D. L.)

LARRABEE. Have you seen this?

MADGE. Yes. Didn't you find Sid?

LARRABEE. No. (*He takes off his coat and hands it to* MADGE *who hangs it up on the coat tree* U. R. *and then moves toward him as he kneels at the safe looking at the dial and examining the lock.*) He wasn't there! We'll have to get a locksmith in.

MADGE. No, no! We can't do that! It isn't safe! (MADGE *sits on the* U. S. L. *side of the ottoman with the newspaper.*)

LARRABEE. We've got to do something, haven't we? There's no time to waste, either! They've put Sherlock Holmes on the case!

MADGE. Sherlock Holmes?

LARRABEE. Yes.

MADGE. What could he do?

LARRABEE. I don't know, but he'll make some move . . . he never waits long!

MADGE. Can't you think of someone else as we can't find Sid?

LARRABEE. He may turn up yet. I left word with Billy Rounds, and he's on the hunt for him. Oh! It's damnable. After holding on for two good years just for this and now the time comes and she's blocked us! Look here! I'll just get at her for a minute. I have an idea I can change her mind.

MADGE. Yes—but wait, Jim. What's the use of hurting the girl? We've tried all that!

LARRABEE. Well, I'll try something else! (*He runs up the stairs onto the balcony.* MADGE *stops him before he opens the* S. L. *door to* ALICE'S *room.*)

MADGE. Jim! Remember . . . nothing that'll show! No marks!

LARRABEE. I'll look out for that. (*He opens the door to* ALICE'S *room and exits closing the door behind him.* MADGE *moves down to the ottoman, picks up the newspaper and reads as she sits.* TERESE *enters from the*

U. C. L. *door that goes to the kitchen. She closes the
door behind her and moves to the* D. S. R. *side of
the ottoman keeping her distance from* MADGE *who is
seated on the* D. C. R. *side of the ottoman.* MADGE *holds
a moment before speaking to* TERESE.)

MADGE. Come here. (TERESE *doesn't move.*) Come
here! (TERESE *moves closer to* MADGE.) Now, what is
it?

TERESE. Meester Judson said I vas to come. (TERESE
avoid looking at MADGE.)

MADGE. I told Judson to arrange with you himself.

TERESE. He could not, madame. I do not veesh
longer to remain.

MADGE. What is it? You must give me some reason!

TERESE. It is zat I wish to go.

MADGE. You've been here months, and have made no
complaint.

TERESE. Ah, madame, it is not so before! It is now
beginning zat I do not like.

MADGE. What? What is it you do not like?

TERESE. I do not like eet, Madame . . . eet . . .
here . . . zis place . . . what you do . . . ze young
lady you have up zere! I cannot remain to see! Eet
eez not well! I cannot remain to see! (MADGE *stands
and moves toward* TERESE.)

MADGE. You know nothing about it! The young lady
is ill. She is not right here. (MADGE *touches her own
forehead.*) She is a great trouble to us, but we take
every care of her and treat her with the utmost kind-
ness . . . (ALICE *screams "AHHHHH!" from off left.*)
Don't be alarmed, my dear, poor Miss Faulkner's head
is very bad today. But she'll be better soon. (ALICE
screams "Nooooo!" and is muffled by something.)
Wait here. (MADGE *runs up the stairs to the balcony.*
FORMAN *enters as* MADGE *gets halfway up the stairs
but holds his position by the* U. C. L. *door.* TERESE
starts to move toward him when MADGE *comes to the
balcony rail and looks down at her.*) Don't leave the

room. (MADGE *exits* S. L. *into* ALICE'S *room.* FORMAN *goes to* TERESE *and they move* D. S. L. *of the round table* S. R. C. *He speaks to her in a low voice.*)

FORMAN. She's made it quite satisfactory, I suppose. You will not leave her now?

TERESE. I can find another place; eet eez not so difficult.

FORMAN. Not so difficult if you know where to go?

TERESE. Ah, zhat eez it!

FORMAN. Here . . . on this card . . . (*Taking a card from his pocket and pushing it into her hands.*) Go to that address! Don't let anyone see it! (TERESE *looks at the card, and reads loudly . . .*)

TERESE. Meester Sheer-lock . . .

FORMAN. (*Covering her mouth with his hand.*) Someone might hear you! Go to that address in the morning. (*The front door bell rings off* U. R. FORMAN *motions her off and she exits through the* U. L. C. *door.* FORMAN *exits* U. R. *to open the house door. SOUND OF THE DOOR CLOSING and* SIDNEY PRINCE *enters carrying a large leather satchel and wearing an overcoat and hat. He is well dressed, moves quickly and is always on the alert.* FORMAN *follows him on.*)

PRINCE. Don't waste toime, you fool; tell 'em as it's Mr. Sidney Prince, Esq. (PRINCE *moves down to the desk putting his satchel on the chair near the desk.*)

FORMAN. Oh yes, sir . . . I beg your *pardon!* I'll announce you immediate, sir. (FORMAN *exits upstairs as* PRINCE *looks about and finds the safe in the desk. He then opens satchel, removes stethescope, puts it on, tests it.*)

PRINCE. Ah! (MADGE *and* LARRABEE *enter onto the balcony* U. L. LARRABEE *closes the door to* ALICE'S *room. He and* MADGE *come down the stairs as* PRINCE *drops to one knee and checks the lock of the safe.*)

MADGE. Oh, is that you, Sid? I'm so glad you've come.

LARRABEE. Hello, Sid.

PRINCE. Larrabee . . .

LARRABEE. Shut up! For Heaven's sake, Sid, remember, *my* name is Chetwood here.

PRINCE. Beg your pardon. My mistake. Old times when we was learnin' the trade together, eh!

LARRABEE. Yes, yes!

PRINCE. I 'ardly expected you'd be doing the 'igh tone thing over 'ere, when I first come up with you workin' the card tables on the Carmania out of New York.

LARRABEE. We don't have to go into that now.

PRINCE. There's no need to get so 'uffy about it! All clear, you say? No danger lurking?

LARRABEE. Not the least! (PRINCE *turns and kneels in front of the safe then stands and faces* LARRABEE.)

PRINCE. You're not robbing *yourselves*, I trust?

LARRABEE. It does look a little like it!

PRINCE. I knew you was on some rum lay, squatting down in this place for over a year; but I never could seem to get a line on you. (PRINCE *turns and kneels in front of the safe then stands and faces* LARRABEE *again.*) What do we get here? It's not 50,000 in used pound notes, by any chance?

LARRABEE. Sorry to disappoint you, but it isn't.

PRINCE. That's too bad. Papers!

LARRABEE. Yes.

PRINCE. Now 'ere . . . (PRINCE *turns and kneels at the safe again and then stands and faces* LARRABEE.) Before we starts 'er going however, what's the general surroundin's?

LARRABEE. What's the good of wasting time on that?

PRINCE. If I'm in this, I'm in it, ain't I? And I want to know wot I'm in.

MADGE. Why don't you tell him, Jimmie?

PRINCE. If anything 'appened, 'ow'd I let the office know 'oo to look out for?

LARRABEE. You know we've been working the Continent. Pleasure places and all that.

PRINCE. So I've heard.

LARRABEE. It was over there . . . Bad Homburg in Bohemia. We ran across a young girl who'd been havin' trouble. Sister just died, no parents. Madge took hold and found that this sister of hers had been having some kind of love affair with a . . . well . . . with a foreign gentleman of exceedingly high rank . . .

PRINCE. A foreign gentleman?

LARRABEE. That's what I said.

PRINCE. 'Ow much was there to it?

LARRABEE. Promise of marriage.

PRINCE. Broke it, of course.

LARRABEE. Yes, and her heart with it. I don't know what more she expected . . . anyway, she did expect more. She and her child died together.

PRINCE. Oh . . . dead!

LARRABEE. Yes, but the case isn't; there's evidence . . . letters, photographs, jewellery with inscriptions that he gave her. The sister's been keeping them . . . We've been keeping the sister . . . You see?

PRINCE. An' what's 'er little game?

LARRABEE. To get even.

PRINCE. An' your little game?

LARRABEE. Whatever there is in it.

PRINCE. These papers an' things ought to be worth a little something!

LARRABEE. I tell you it wouldn't be safe for him to marry until he gets them out of the way! He knows it very well. But what's more, the *family* knows it!

PRINCE. Oh . . . family! Rich, I take it.

LARRABEE. Rich isn't quite the word. They're something else. (LARRABEE *whispers into* PRINCE'S *ear*.)

PRINCE. . . . My Gawd! Royalty itself, eh? Which one of 'em?

LARRABEE. I can't tell you that.

PRINCE. Well, we ARE a-movin' among the swells now, ain't we? But this 'ere girl, the sister o' the one that died . . . 'ow did you manage to get 'er into it?

MADGE. I picked her up of course and consoled her. I invited her to stay with me at my house in London. Jimmy came over and took this place . . . and when I brought her along a week later it was all ready . . . and a private desk safe for the letters and jewellery.

LARRABEE. Yes, combination, lock and all. Everything worked smooth until a couple of weeks ago, when we began to hear from a firm of London solicitors, some veiled proposals were made. Which showed that the time was coming. They wanted the things out of the way. Suddenly all negotiations on their side stopped. The next thing for me to do was to threaten. I wanted the letters for this, but when I went to get them, I found that in some way the girl had managed to change the lock on us. The numbers were wrong and we couldn't frighten or starve her into opening the thing.

PRINCE. You've got the stuff in there!

LARRABEE. That's what I'm telling you, it's in there and she juggled the lock.

PRINCE. Oh, well, it won't take long to rectify that triflin' error. (PRINCE *kneels at the safe then stands again.*) But wot puzzles *me* is why the solicitors broke off with their offers that way. (MADGE *moves* U. C. R. *to the round table and adjusts the newspaper.*)

LARRABEE. That's simple enough. They've given it up themselves and got in Sherlock Holmes.

PRINCE. Wot's that? Is 'Olmes in this?

LARRABEE. That's what they told me!

MADGE. But what can he *do*, Sid? (PRINCE *moves* U. S. L. *to the* D. S. *end of the piano and takes out a notebook and pencil. He writes a message.*)

PRINCE. 'Ere, don't stand talking about that . . . I'll get the safe open. You send a telegram, that's all I want! Where's your nearest telegraph office?

MADGE. Round the corner. (PRINCE *tears out a page from the notebook folds it and hands it to* LARRABEE.)

PRINCE. Run for it! Mind what I say . . . *run for it.* That's to Alf Bassick. He's Professor Moriarty's confidential man. Moriarty is king in London. He runs everything that's shady and 'Olmes 'as been settin' lines all round 'im for months and he didn't know it . . . an' now he's beginning to find out that 'Olmes is trackin' him down and there's the devil to pay.

LARRABEE. What are you telling him?

PRINCE. Nothing whatever, except I've got a job on as I wants to see 'im about in the morning. Read it yourself. But don't take all night over it! You can't tell wot might 'appen.

MADGE. Go on, Jim!

LARRABEE. Keep your eyes open.

MADGE. Don't you worry! (LARRABEE *runs off* U. R. *There is the* SOUND OF THE FRONT DOOR CLOSING. MADGE *moves* U. C. *to watch* LARRABEE *leave then she moves* D. S. C. *and sits on the* S. R. *side of the ottoman watching* PRINCE *layout his tools* D. S. L. *in front of the desk.*) I've heard of this Professor Moriarty. What does he do?

PRINCE. I'll tell you one thing he does! He's the Emperor! He sits at 'ome, quiet and easy, an' runs nearly every big operation that's on. (PRINCE *works on the safe with some of his tools.*) All the clever boys are under him one way or another an' he holds them in his hand without moving a muscle! And if there's a slip and the police get wind of it, there ain't never any hold on him. They can't touch him. And wot's more, they wouldn't want to do it if they could.

MADGE. Why not? (PRINCE *puts the tools he has been working with down and picks up the drill and puts it on the safe lock.*)

PRINCE. Because they've tried it, that's why. And the men as did try it was found shortly after a-floatin' in the river, that is, if they was found at all! The moment a man's marked by Moriarty, there ain't a street that's safe for him! (PRINCE *drills on the safe door.* MADGE *watches him and then stands.*)

MADGE. Have you got it, Sid?

PRINCE. Not yet, but I'll be there soon. I know where I am now.

(*THE SOUND OF THE FRONT DOOR* U. R. *is heard closing and* LARRABEE *runs on wiping his mouth and breathless from running. He goes to* PRINCE *at the desk.* MADGE *moves toward* LARRABEE *watching* PRINCE.)

LARRABEE. Well, Sid. How goes it?

PRINCE. So-so.

LARRABEE. Now about this Professor Moriarty?

PRINCE. Ask 'er.

MADGE. It's all right, Jim. It was the proper thing to do. (PRINCE *opens the safe door, then stands and moves near the* D. S. *end of the piano so the* LARRABEES *can look into the safe. IT'S EMPTY!* LARRABEE *kneels at the safe looking in then feels inside to make sure there is nothing there.*) Gone!

LARRABEE. She's taken 'em out.

PRINCE. What do you mean?

LARRABEE. The girl! (MADGE *goes to the desk, pulls down the desk top and rummages through the drawers and papers then slams the desk top shut.*)

MADGE. She's got them!

PRINCE. She wants to get even, you say.

MADGE. Yes! Yes!

PRINCE. Well, then, if she's got the things out of the safe there . . . (LARRABEE *paces* U. S. *and* D. S. *on the* S. R. *side.*) ain't it quite likely she's sent 'em along to the girl as 'is Royal Highness wants to marry.

MADGE. No! She hasn't had the chance. (LARRABEE *goes to the round table and opens the* S. L. *drawer then closes it.*)

LARRABEE. She couldn't get them out of this room. We've watched her too close for that. (LARRABEE *starts for the stairs and* PRINCE *moves* C. S.)

MADGE. Wait!

LARRABEE. I'll get her down! She'll tell us where they are or strangle for it! (LARRABEE *runs up the stairs onto the balcony and looks over the balcony rail to* MADGE *and* PRINCE.) Wait here! When I get her down, don't give her time to think! (LARRABEE *opens the door to* ALICE'S *room and exits* S. L. *closing the door behind him.*)

PRINCE. Wot's he goin' to do?

MADGE. We've got to get it out of her or the whole two years' work is wasted. So there's only one thing he can do. (*A muffled scream of "no!!" is heard from* ALICE *off* U. S. L. *Pause.*)

PRINCE. Look 'ere, I don't so much fancy this sort of thing. Torture and that.

MADGE. Don't you worry, we'll attend to it! (PRINCE *moves* D. L. *and wraps his tools up in the cloth he carries them in.*)

PRINCE. Well, I suppose there are more ways to kill a cat then drowning it with cream. If you've got your heart set on it, that is. (PRINCE *picks up the cloth with his tools wrapped up in it and puts it in his satchel on the chair near the desk.*)

MADGE. For two years . . . (*The balcony door* U. S. L. *opens and* LARRABEE *appears pulling* ALICE FAULKNER *out of her room onto the balcony.*)

LARRABEE. Now we'll see whether you will or not. (LARRABEE *swings* ALICE *around grabbing her by the right wrist and pulling her down the stairs and stopping* U. S. C.) Now tell her what we want.

ALICE. You needn't tell me, I know well enough. (MADGE *goes to her and leads her* D. S. L. *near the desk.*)

MADGE. Oh no, dear, you don't know. It isn't anything to do with locks, or keys, or numbers this time.

We want to know what you've done with them! Do you hear! We want to know what you've done with them. (MADGE *grabs* ALICE *by the shoulders and swings her around to face the safe.* ALICE *breaks away from her and runs* S. R. *below the ottoman and starts to go* U. S. *but is blocked by* LARRABEE.)

ALICE. You will not know from me. (LARRABEE *grabs her right hand and spins her around twisting her right arm behind her so that she is facing front.*)

LARRABEE. You're going to tell us what you've done with that package before you leave this room tonight! (LARRABEE *puts more pressure on her arm.*)

ALICE. Not if you kill me.

LARRABEE. It isn't killing that's going to do it. It's something else. (LARRABEE *gives her arm another twist. She gives a slight cry of pain.* PRINCE *appears not to notice what's happening yet doesn't move.*)

MADGE. Tell us where it is! Tell us and he'll stop. (LARRABEE *applies more pressure.*)

LARRABEE. Out with it!

MADGE. *Where is it?*

LARRABEE. Where is it? I'll give you a turn next time that'll take it out of you. Where is it? (LARRABEE *grabs her by the throat.*)

MADGE. Be careful, Jimmie! (LARRABEE *shakes* ALICE *by the throat.*)

LARRABEE. Is this any time to be careful? Will you tell? Will you . . . (*THE FRONT DOORBELL RINGS.*)

PRINCE. LOOK OUT! (FORMAN *enters from* U. C. L. *doorway under the balcony and stands* U. C. . . . *waiting.* ALICE *collapses onto the ottoman.*)

LARRABEE. Here! Don't go to that door. (*To* MADGE.) See who it is. (MADGE *runs* U. R. C. *to the stairs and goes up onto the first landing and looks off* S. R. . . . *PAUSE . . . then she runs down the stairs to* C. S. LARRABEE *moves* ALICE *from the ottoman to the* D. R. *chair.*)

MADGE. Tall, slim man, long coat, soft hat, smooth face, carries an ebony cane!

PRINCE. Sherlock 'Olmes! He's 'ere!

LARRABEE. We won't answer the bell. (LARRABEE *crosses* S. L. *to the piano and turns off the lamp on the* D. S. *end of the piano.*)

PRINCE. No! That man, he's got hypernatural powers! He knows what the rats are thinking in the cellars!

LARRABEE. Nonsense.

PRINCE. Hide the girl. Get her away! Quick!

LARRABEE. Well I suppose if we have to answer the bell . . .

PRINCE. It's your only hope!

LARRABEE. Take her up the back stairway! (MADGE *gets* ALICE *out of the chair* D. R. *forcing her onto her feet and moving her* U. C. L. *toward the passage way* U. L. . . . S. L. *of the doorway to the kitchen.*)

MADGE. She's in poor health and can't see anyone . . . you *understand.* (MADGE *exits quickly with* ALICE U. L.)

LARRABEE. Yes! Yes! Lock her in the room and stay by the door. Sid, you get out there! (LARRABEE *indicates the window behind the desk.*) Keep quiet there till he gets in the house. Then come round to the front. Be ready for 'im when he comes out! If he's got the things in spite of us, I'll give you two sharp whistles! If you don't hear it, let him pass.

PRINCE. But if I *do* 'ear the two whistles? (LARRABEE *opens the* U. S. *top drawer of the desk and takes out a padded metal pipe.*)

LARRABEE. Then let him have it. (LARRABEE *hands the pipe to* PRINCE. PRINCE *holding his satchel in his hand and pipe in his other hand steps onto the desk chair, then onto the* U. S. *top drawer which* LARRABEE *has left open, and onto the top of the desk.* LARRABEE *quickly grabs a photograph out of* PRINCE'S *way as* PRINCE *steps up onto the top of the desk and steps out the window.* LARRABEE *puts the photograph back into its position once* PRINCE *has passed.* LARRABEE *closes the window and re-adjusts the curtains.* FORMAN *is still standing* U. S. C. LARRABEE *turns to him. THE DOOR BELL IS STILL HEARD RINGING.)* Go on, answer the bell. (FORMAN *bows slightly and exits* U. S. R. LARRABEE *checks the window and the desk. THE SOUND OF THE FRONT DOOR IS HEARD CLOSING.* LARRABEE *picks up a cigar and box of matches from the* D. S. *end of the piano and continues to look out of the window as* SHERLOCK HOLMES *enters wearing a long coat, gloves, hat and carrying an ebony cane.* HOLMES *moves slowly* D. R. C. *stopping* S. R. *of the round table.* FORMAN *bows and goes up the stairs, stopping on the balcony just before he opens the door to* ALICE'S *room.* FORMAN *watches* HOLMES *for a few moments.* LARRABEE *lights his cigar.* HOLMES *stands for several seconds with his coat open and his left hand on his hip; then he puts his hat and cane down on the* S. L. *side of the table. He starts to take off his left glove and* FORMAN *exits* U. S. L. *closing the balcony door which cues* LARRABEE *to turn to* HOLMES.) Mr. Holmes, I believe. (HOLMES *takes off his right glove and turns to* LARRABEE.)

HOLMES. Yes, sir.

LARRABEE. Who did you wish to see, Mr. Holmes? (HOLMES *puts his gloves on the table.*)

HOLMES. Thank you so much . . . (HOLMES *crosses* D. S. R. *to the chair.*) I sent my card by the butler. (HOLMES *sits in the* D. S. R. *chair.* LARRABEE *moves* D. S. *slightly.*)

LARRABEE. Oh, very well.

(*There is a long pause as* FORMAN *enters onto the balcony* U. S. L., *closes the door and comes down the stairs, stopping* C. S. *above the ottoman.* HOLMES *takes out his card case, calling card and pencil from his right pocket and jots down a note on the calling card.* HOLMES *crosses his legs.*)

FORMAN. Miss Faulkner begs Mr. Holmes to excuse her. She is not well enough to see anyone this evening. (FORMAN *and* LARRABEE *watch* HOLMES. HOLMES *finishes writing and puts the card case and pencil back into his pocket as he offers his calling card to* FORMAN.)

HOLMES. Hand Miss Faulkner this and say, that I have— (FORMAN *steps toward* HOLMES *to take the card but stops on* LARRABEE'S *next line.*)

LARRABEE. I beg your pardon, Mr. Holmes, but it's quite useless really.

HOLMES. Oh, I'm so sorry to hear it. (HOLMES *looks at* LARRABEE.)

LARRABEE. Yes, Miss Faulkner is, I regret to say, quite an *invalid.* She is unable to see anyone; her health is so poor.

HOLMES. Did it ever occur to you that she might be confined to the house too much?

LARRABEE. How does that concern you? (LARRABEE *puts his cigar in his mouth.*)

HOLMES. It doesn't, I simply made the suggestion. (HOLMES *stands and gives his card to* FORMAN.) That's all. Go on. Take it up. (FORMAN *goes up the stairs and exits* U. S. L. *into* ALICE'S *room closing the door behind him.* HOLMES *takes off his coat and goes* U. R. *to the coat tree and hangs it up then comes* D. C. *checking his cuff links.* LARRABEE *leans on the back of the desk chair* S. L. HOLMES *moves back to the* D. R. *chair.*)

LARRABEE. Ha! Ha! Well, of *course* he can take up your card or your note . . . or whatever it is, if you wish it so much; I was only trying to save you the trouble.

HOLMES. Thanks . . . (HOLMES *picks up the newspaper that is on the* D. S. *end of the round table* S. R., *opens it as he sits in the* D. R. *chair and reads.*) . . . hardly any trouble at all to send a card.

LARRABEE. Do you know, Mr. Holmes, you interest me very much. (HOLMES *continues to read the paper.*)

HOLMES. Ah! (LARRABEE *crosses* C. *above the otto-man.*)

LARRABEE. Upon my word, yes! We've all heard of your wonderful methods. Your marvellous insight, your ingenuity in picking up and following clues; and the astonishing manner in which you gain information from the most trifling details. Now, I dare say, in this brief moment or two you've discovered any number of things about me. (HOLMES *still holds the newspaper open as if he's reading it and crosses his legs.*)

HOLMES. Nothing of consequence, Mr. Chetwood, I have scarcely more than asked myself why you rushed off and sent that telegram in such a frightened hurry, what possible excuse you could have had for gulping down that tumbler of raw brandy at the "Lion Head" on the way back, why your friend left so suddenly by the terrace window, and what there can possibly be about the safe in the lower part of that desk to cause you such painful anxiety. (*Pause.* LARRABEE *breaks into laughter.*)

LARRABEE. Ha! Ha! Very good! (FORMAN *opens the balcony door and comes down stairs.*) Very good indeed! If those things were only true now, I'd be wonderfully impressed. (FORMAN *comes down to him holding a salver with a note on it.* LARRABEE *takes the note.*) You will excuse me, I trust. (*He opens the note and reads it.* HOLMES *continues to look at the newspaper.*) Ah, it's from . . . er . . . Miss Faulkner! Well really! She begs to be allowed to see Mr. Holmes. She absolutely *implores* it! Well, I suppose I shall have to give way. Judson!

FORMAN. Sir.

LARRABEE. *Ask Miss Faulkner* to come down to the drawing room. Say that Mr. Holmes is waiting to see her.

FORMAN. Yes, sir. (FORMAN *still holding the salver takes the note back from him and goes up the stairs and exits* U. L. *closing the balcony door behind him.*)

LARRABEE. This is quite remarkable, upon my soul! May I ask, if it's not an impertinent question, what message you sent up that could have so aroused Miss Faulkner's desire to come down?

HOLMES. Merely that if she wasn't down in five minutes, I'd go up.

LARRABEE. Oh, that was it! (LARRABEE *puts his cigar in his mouth.*)

HOLMES. Quite so. And unless I'm very much mistaken, I hear the young lady on the stairs. (HOLMES *folds the paper and places it back onto the round table as he stands and takes out his watch.*) In which case she has one and one-half minutes to spare. (*He looks at his watch and puts it away as he crosses* S. L. *to the piano. The BALCONY door opens and* MADGE LARRABEE *appears. She closes the door and comes down the stairs.* LARRABEE *puts his cigar in the ashtray on the* D. S. *end of the piano and crosses* U. C. *to meet her. He gives her his arm as she comes down the last few steps; and helps her to* HOLMES U. S. C. *She gives the impression of being a little weak but endeavors not to let it be seen. It is optional, but as* MADGE *gets half way down the stairs, she starts coughing and tries to cover it by putting her handkerchief to her mouth.*)

LARRABEE. Alice, or that is, Miss Faulkner, (*Optional, she coughs again.*) let me introduce Mr. Sherlock Holmes. (MADGE *extends her hand to* HOLMES *which he takes.*)

HOLMES. Miss Faulkner!

MADGE. Mr. Holmes, I'm really most charmed to meet you, I was more than anxious to come down, only the doctor has forbidden my seeing anyone; but when Cousin Freddie said that I might come, of course that placed the responsibility on him, so I have a perfectly clear conscience.

HOLMES. I thank you very much indeed for consenting to see me, Miss Faulkner, but I regret that you were put to the trouble of making such a very rapid change of dress.

MADGE. Oh, not at all, Mr. Holmes, you see, during the day, I am allowed to get up and sit by the window.

HOLMES. And you were up sitting looking out of the window.

MADGE. Yes. (HOLMES *turns* S. L. *checking the piano.*)

HOLMES. Admiring the fog? (*Optional,* MADGE *coughs. She moves* D. L. *to the* S. L. *chair in front of the desk as* HOLMES *counters with her* D. R. *to the chair.*)

MADGE. Mr. Holmes is quite living up to his reputation, isn't he, Freddie? (*She sits at the desk chair; and* HOLMES *sits in the* D. R. *chair clasping his hands in his lap.*)

LARRABEE. Well, I don't know about that. (LARRABEE *moves to the* D. S. *end of the piano and picks up his cigar.*)

MADGE. Oh, has he been making mistakes? I'm so sorry!

LARRABEE. He's been telling me the most astonishing things.

MADGE. And they weren't true?

LARRABEE. Listen to this one. He wanted to know what there was about the safe in that desk that caused me such anxiety. Ha! Ha! Ha!

MADGE. Why there isn't anything. Is there?

LARRABEE. That's just it! There's a good safe there, but nothing in it.

MADGE. My goodness, I wonder what it was Mr. Holmes thought we had in there!

LARRABEE. Perhaps you'll do better next time!

MADGE. Yes, next time, you might try on me, Mr. Holmes.

LARRABEE. Yes, what do you think of her? (LARRABEE *stands* U. S. *of* MADGE.)

HOLMES. It is very easy to discern one thing about Miss Faulkner; and that is, that she is particularly fond of the piano, that her touch is exquisite, her expression wonderful, and her technique extraordinary. While she likes light music well enough, she is extremely fond of Chopin, Liszt and Brahms. She plays a great deal, indeed; I see it is her chief diversion, which makes it all the more remarkable *that she has not touched* (*He looks at* MADGE.) *the piano for three days.* (MADGE *turns to* LARRABEE *and laughs.*)

MADGE. Why, that's quite surprising, isn't it? (LARRABEE *moves betwen the* D. S. *end of the piano and the* U. S. *end of the desk.*)

LARRABEE. Certainly better than he did for me. (HOLMES *gets up and crosses* C. *above the ottoman.*)

HOLMES. I am glad somewhat to repair my shattered reputation, and as a reward will Miss Faulkner be so good as to play me something of which I am particularly fond.

MADGE. I shall be delighted, if I *can.* (LARRABEE *leans on the* D. S. *end of the piano.* HOLMES *turns* S. R. *checking the* D. R. *chair.*)

HOLMES. If you can! (*Facing front.*) Something tells me that Chopin's Prelude Number Seven is at your fingers' ends. (*He turns to* MADGE.)

MADGE. Oh yes! I can give you *that.* (HOLMES *offers his hand to* MADGE *to help her up from the chair.* LARRABEE *also helps by taking her other arm.* HOLMES *and* MADGE *moves* U. C. *near the* U. S. *end of the piano.*)

HOLMES. It will please me so much. (*Optional,* MADGE *coughs.*)

MADGE. Tell me, Mr. Holmes, how did you know so much about my playing . . . my expression . . . technique. (HOLMES *takes hold of her hand.*)

HOLMES. Miss Faulkner's hands. (*She takes her hand away.*)

MADGE. And my preference for the composers you mentioned?

HOLMES. The music-rack.

MADGE. How simple! But you said I hadn't played for three days. How did . . .

HOLMES. The keys.

MADGE. The keys?

HOLMES. A light layer of dust. (LARRABEE *puts his cigar in his mouth;* MADGE *moves behind the piano and dusts the keys lightly with her handkerchief.* HOLMES *turns* U. S. L. *checking the servants entrance area.*)

MADGE. Dust! Oh dear! I never knew Térèse to forget before. You must think us very untidy, I'm sure, Mr. Holmes. (HOLMES *turns to face her.*)

HOLMES. On the contrary. I see from many things that you are not untidy in the least, and I am therefore compelled to conclude that the failure of Térèse is due to something else.

MADGE. Wh—what? (HOLMES *faces front.*)

HOLMES. To some unusual excitement or disturbance that has recently taken place (*Looks at* MADGE.) in this house. (LARRABEE *puts his cigar back into his mouth.*)

MADGE. You are doing very well, Mr. Holmes, and you deserve your Chopin. (*She sits at the piano and prepares to play.* HOLMES *moves* S. R. *to the tower where the bell-pull is and stands with his back to it.*)

HOLMES. Thanks.

(MADGE *has a practice run during which* HOLMES *pulls the bell-pull and moves* C. S. MADGE *picks up the piece of music she is to play and arranges it on the music rack. She plays.* LARRABEE *moves along side the* S. L. *side of the piano.* HOLMES *moves to the* D. R. *side of the ottoman. On the second phrase of music,* HOLMES *falls onto the ottoman sideways.* FORMAN *enters from the servant's door* U. L. *closing it behind him. He moves to the* U. C. R. *position.* LARRABEE *sees him and moves up to* MADGE *and whispers to her as she continues to play.* MADGE *looks up, sees* FORMAN *and stops playing.*)

MADGE. What are you doing here, Judson?

FORMAN. I came to see what was wanted, ma'am.

MADGE. What was wanted? (LARRABEE *crosses* U. S. *of* MADGE *who remains seated at the piano and goes to* FORMAN.)

LARRABEE. Nobody asked you to come here.

FORMAN. I beg your pardon, sir. I answered the bell.

LARRABEE. What bell?

FORMAN. The drawing-room bell, sir.

LARRABEE. What do you mean, you blockhead?

FORMAN. I'm quite sure it rung, sir.

LARRABEE. Well, I tell you it did *not* ring! (HOLMES *is still seated on the ottoman facing front.*)

HOLMES. Your butler is right, Mr. Chetwood, the bell *did* ring.

LARRABEE. How do you know?

HOLMES. I rang it. (LARRABEE *moves* S. L. *toward the* D. S. *end of the piano and* MADGE *stands up.*)

LARRABEE. What do you want. (HOLMES *gets up and moves* U. C. *between* FORMAN *and* MADGE *holding out his calling card to* FORMAN.)

HOLMES. I want to send my card to Miss Faulkner. (HOLMES *still holds the card out for* FORMAN *to take.*)

LARRABEE. What right have you to ring for servants and give orders in my house? (HOLMES *turns to* LARRABEE *but holds the card out for* FORMAN.)

HOLMES. And what right have you to prevent my cards from reaching their destination; and how does it happen that you and this woman are resorting to trickery and deceit to prevent me from seeing Alice Faulkner? (*He turns back to* FORMAN.) Through some trifling oversight, Judson, neither of the cards that I handed you has been delivered. See that this *error* does not occur again. (*He hands the card to* FORMAN.)

FORMAN. My orders, sir . . .

HOLMES. Oh, you have orders?

FORMAN. I can't say, sir, as I . . . (HOLMES *turns to* MADGE *and* LARRABEE.)

HOLMES. You were told not to deliver my card!

LARRABEE. What business is this of yours? I'd like to know?

HOLMES. I shall satisfy your curiosity on that point in a very short time.

LARRABEE. Yes, and you'll find out in a very short time that it isn't safe to meddle with me! It wouldn't be any trouble for me to throw you out into the street.

HOLMES. Quite possibly not . . . but trouble would swiftly follow such an experiment on your part. (LARRABEE *moves toward* HOLMES.)

LARRABEE. It's a cursed lucky thing for you I'm not armed. (HOLMES *moves toward* LARRABEE.)

HOLMES. Yes, well, when Miss Faulkner comes down you can go and arm yourself. (HOLMES *turns and moves* U. C.)

LARRABEE. Arm myself! (*He moves* D. L. *and then back to the* D. S. *end of the piano.*) I'll call the police! And what's more, I'll do it now. (LARRABEE *starts to go* U. C. *but is stopped by* MADGE *as he passes her.* HOLMES *turns to* LARRABEE.)

HOLMES. You will not do it now. You will remain where you are until the young lady I came here to see has entered this room.

LARRABEE. What makes you so sure of that?

HOLMES. Because you will infinitely prefer to avoid an investigation of your very suspicious conduct, Mr. James Larrabee. (FORMAN, LARRABEE *and* MADGE *step back.*) An investigation that will certainly take place if you or your wife presume further to interfere with my business. (*He turns to* FORMAN.) As for you, my man, it gives me great pleasure to recall the features of an old acquaintance. Your recent connection with the signing of another man's name (FORMAN *faces front.*) to a small piece of paper has made your presence at Bow Street much desired. You will either deliver that card to Miss Faulkner at once—or you sleep in the police station tonight. (HOLMES *moves* D. R. *and stands with his back to* LARRABEE *and*

MADGE.) It is a matter of small consequence to me which you do. (FORMAN *crosses to* LARRABEE *holding out* HOLMES' *calling card.*)

FORMAN. Shall I go, sir?

LARRABEE. Go on. Take up the card. (FORMAN *exits up the stairs and out through the balcony door closing it behind him.* LARRABEE *and* MADGE *move* D. L.) It makes no difference to me. (*Aside to* LARRABEE.)

MADGE. If she comes down can't he get them away from her?

LARRABEE. If he does, Sid Prince is waiting for him outside.

(HOLMES *turns to face* U. L. *with his hands behind him to watch* ALICE FAULKNER *enter onto the balcony.* LARRABEE *moves up to the* D. S. *end of the piano;* MADGE *moves to the* U. S. *side of the desk chair and puts her hand on the back of it. All three watch as* ALICE *enters onto the balcony, closing the door behind her, and coming down the stairs stopping* U. C. *PAUSE.* HOLMES *crosses slowly* S. L. *toward* LARRABEE *and* MADGE. ALICE *moves* D. S. *near the* S. L. *side of the round table.*)

HOLMES. A short time since you displayed an acute anxiety to leave the room. Pray do not let me detain you or your wife any longer. (ALICE *moves to the* U. S. R. *side of the ottoman and turns to face* HOLMES. MADGE *sits in the desk chair;* LARRABEE *holds his position at the* D. S. *end of the piano.* HOLMES *turns to face* ALICE.)

ALICE. This is Mr. Holmes?

HOLMES. Yes.

ALICE. You wished to see me?

HOLMES. Very much indeed, Miss Faulkner, but I am sorry to see you are far from well.

ALICE. Oh, no . . .

HOLMES. No? (*Takes her right hand and pushes the*

sleeve of her blouse back exposing her wrist.) I beg
your pardon, but . . . what does this mean?

ALICE. Oh, nothing. (HOLMES *lets go of her hand.*)

HOLMES. Nothing!

ALICE. No!

HOLMES. And the mark here on your neck plainly
showing the clutch of a man's fingers? Does that mean
nothing also? (*Faces front.*) It occurs to me that I
would like to have an explanation of this. Possibly,
you can furnish one, Mr. Larrabee? (LARRABEE *moves
slightly* D. S.)

LARRABEE. How should I know?

HOLMES. It seems to have occurred in your house.

LARRABEE. What if it did? (*Moving toward* HOLMES.)
You'd better understand that it isn't healthy for you
or anyone else to interfere with my business. (HOLMES
turns to LARRABEE.)

HOLMES. Ah! Then it is your business. We have that
much at least. (HOLMES *turns back to* ALICE *and moves*
S. R. *to move the* D. R. *chair closer to the ottoman.*)
Pray be seated, Miss Faulkner. (*She turns to him.*)

ALICE. I don't know who you are, Mr. Holmes, or
why you are here.

HOLMES. I shall be very glad to answer that question. So far as my identity is concerned, you have my
name and address as well as the announcement of my
profession inscribed upon the card, which I observe
you still hold clasped tightly in the fingers of your
left hand.

ALICE. (*She looks at the card.*) A . . . detective!
(HOLMES *offers her the* D. R. *chair but she sits on the*
U. S. R. *side of the ottoman instead.*)

HOLMES. Quite so. And my business is this. (*He sits
in the chair and leans toward her.*) I have been consulted as to the possibility of obtaining from you certain letters and other things which are supposed to be
in your possession, and which, I need not tell you, are
the source of the greatest anxiety.

ALICE. It is quite true I have such letters, Mr. Holmes, but it will be impossible to get them from me; others have tried and failed.

HOLMES. What others have or have not done, whilst possibly instructive in certain directions, can in no way affect my conduct, Miss Faulkner. I have come to you frankly and directly, to beg you to pity and forgive.

ALICE. There are some things, Mr. Holmes, beyond pity, beyond forgiveness.

HOLMES. But there are other things that are not. I am able to assure you of the sincere penitence, the deep regret, of the one who inflicted the injury, and of his earnest desire to make any reparation in his power.

ALICE. How can reparation be made to the dead? (HOLMES *faces front with his hands clasped in his lap.*)

HOLMES. How indeed! And by the very same token any injury you may yourself be able to inflict by means of these things can be no reparation, no satisfaction, no indemnity to the one who is no longer here. You will be acting for the living . . . not the dead. For your own satisfaction, Miss Faulkner, your own gratification and your own revenge! (*She gets up and goes* U. C. *and turns back to him. He gets up immediately after she does and moves to the* S. R. *side of the round table* U. S. *of the* D. R. *chair.*)

ALICE. I know from this and from other things that have happened . . . that a marriage is contemplated.

HOLMES. It is quite true. (HOLMES *watches her as he puts his right hand on the back of the* D. R. *chair.*)

ALICE. I *cannot* give up what I intend to do, Mr. Holmes. There are other things beside revenge. There is punishment. If I am not able to communicate with the family to which this man proposes to ally himself . . . in time to prevent such a thing . . . the punishment will come later . . . but you may be perfectly sure it will come. There is nothing more to say! Good night, Mr. Holmes. (HOLMES *stamps his foot on the floor three times as a signal for the explosion in the kitchen.*)

HOLMES. But, my dear Miss Faulkner, before you . . . (*Confused noise, shouting and screams are heard from off* U. L. *along with an explosion and crash followed by smoke. Everyone stops and listens.*)

TERESE. (*Off Stage* U. L.) Au secours, mon Dieu, au secours! (TERESE *continues to ad lib while* FORMAN *enters from* U. C. L. *followed by smoke pouring out of the passageway. He moves* D. S. C.)

FORMAN. Mr. Chetwood! Mr. Chetwood!

MADGE and LARRABEE. What is it?

FORMAN. The lamp in the kitchen, sir! It fell off the table and everything down there is blazing, sir.

(*BEAT before anyone moves.* ALICE *is the first to move. She starts quickly* D. S. R. *toward the chair.* HOLMES *moves* U. R. C. *near the bell-pull and watches* ALICE. *She stops and quickly goes to the ottoman and grabs the two pillows off the ottoman and clutches them to her.* FORMAN, LARRABEE *and* MADGE *run* U. S. L. *and exit through the* U. C. L. *door to the kitchen.* MADGE *closes the door behind her.* TERESE *is still heard shouting.* ALICE *stands facing the desk* S. L.)

MADGE. The house is on fire! Terese, keep calm. Keep calm, Terese. (*The sound of* TERESE *being slapped is heard then silence.* HOLMES *moves* D. C. *to* ALICE.)

HOLMES. Don't alarm yourself, Miss Faulkner . . . there is no fire. (*As she turns to him, he takes the pillows from her one at a time and drops them onto the ottoman.*)

ALICE. No fire!

HOLMES. The smoke was all arranged for by me. (*He moves to the* D. R. *chair, kneels in front of it feel-*

*ing of the seat; then he tears off the fabric upholstered
onto the seat and takes out the packet of letters hidden
in the seat.)*

ALICE. Arranged for? (*She starts to go* U. L. C. *then
turns back to* HOLMES.) What does this mean, Mr.
Holmes? (*She runs* D. R. *of the round table stopping
behind the* D. R. *chair just as* HOLMES *stands up with
the packet of letters and moves* C. S. *above the ottoman.* ALICE *moves* C. S. *making a grab for the packet
which* HOLMES *holds in his left hand. It is out of her
reach.)*

HOLMES. That I wanted this package of letters,
Miss Faulkner . . . (ALICE *looks at* HOLMES *and
then collapses onto the ottoman as* HOLMES *turns and
picks up his coat from the coat stand* U. R. *He throws
the coat over his right arm and moves down to the*
S. L. *side of the round table for his gloves, hat and
cane. He picks up his gloves then notices* ALICE *and
puts his gloves down.)* I will not take them, Miss
Faulkner. (*He puts his gloves back on the table and
moves sligthly* D. R. *She sits up and looks at him.)*
As you very likely conjecture, the alarm of fire was
only to make you betray their hiding-place . . . which
you did . . . and I availed myself of that betrayal,
as you see. But now that I witness your great distress,
I find I cannot take them, unless . . . (*He drops onto
his* D. S. *knee facing her.)* you can possibly change
your mind and let me have them of your own free
will. (*She shakes her head slightly. He stands.)* I
hardly supposed you could. (*She makes a slight move
for the packet.)* I will therefore . . . (*He holds the
packet up toward* ALICE *when* LARRABEE *enters from*
U. C. L. *holding a revolver.* MADGE *is behind him. He
moves* D. C. *pointing the revolver toward* HOLMES.)

LARRABEE. So! You've got them, have you? And
now, I suppose we're going to see you walk out of the
house with them. (HOLMES *starts to move toward*
ALICE *then steps back.)*

HOLMES. On the contrary, you're going to see me return them to their rightful owner.

LARRABEE. Yes, I think that will be the safest thing for Mr. Sherlock Holmes to do. (HOLMES *puts the package down to his side.*)

HOLMES. You flatter yourself, Mr. Larrabee. The reason that I do not leave the house with this package of papers is not because of you, or what you may do, or say, or think, or feel! It is solely on account of this young lady! (HOLMES *moves* C. S. *above* ALICE *who is sitting with her back to the audience on the ottoman.* LARRABEE *and* MADGE *move* U. S. LARRABEE *to the* U. S. R. *side of the piano;* MADGE *just behind the keyboard of the piano near* LARRABEE. HOLMES *speaks to* ALICE *while* LARRABEE *still holds the revolver pointed at* HOLMES' *back.*) It is a matter of constant regret to me, Miss Faulkner that my chosen profession involves me with an underworld most of whose members are not gentlemen. But although Mr. Larrabee may not understand honor, I feel sure that you do. Allow me to place this in your hands. (HOLMES *gives the package to* ALICE.) Should you ever change your mind and be so generous and so forgiving, as to wish to return these letters to the one who wrote them, you have my address. In any event, rest assured there will be no more cruelty, no more persecution in this house. You are perfectly safe with your property now, for I have so arranged it that your faintest cry of distress will be heard! (HOLMES *turns and goes* U. S. R. *toward the bell pull on the tower and turns back to her motioning her to leave.*) Good night, Miss Faulkner. (ALICE *stands and goes* U. C. *to the stairs.* LARRABEE *moves* D. S. L. *a bit to let her pass.* ALICE *runs up the stairs to the balcony and pauses looking at* HOLMES *before she exits* U. L. *into her room closing the door behind her.* HOLMES, MADGE *and* LARRABEE *watch her exit. Beat.* HOLMES *crosses* S. L. *and taps* LARRABEE *on the shoulder.* LARRABEE *and* MADGE *both turn to face*

HOLMES.) As for you, sir, and you, madam, I beg you to understand that you continue your persecution of that young lady *at your peril.* (HOLMES *turns* S. R. *and goes to the round table picking up his gloves, cane and hat.* HOLMES *starts to exit* U. R. *but stops and comes back toward the* LARRABEES. *Beat.*) Good evening. (HOLMES *turns* S. R. *putting his hat on and exits* U. S. R. *There is the sound of the front door closing* U. S. R. *Beat.* SIDNEY PRINCE *appears at the window* S. L. *and climbs into the room.*)

PRINCE. Well! 'E didn't get the stuff, did 'e?

MADGE. He gave it to *her.* (LARRABEE *crosses* R. C. *and paces* U. S. *and* D. S.)

PRINCE. What! 'E found it? And gave it to the girl? Well 'ere, I say! Wot are you waiting for? Now's the chance before she hides it again! (PRINCE *moves* C. S. *as* LARRABEE *starts for the stairs.*)

MADGE. No! Wait!

PRINCE. Wot's the matter! Do you want to lose it?

LARRABEE. No! You're right! It's all a cursed bluff! (LARRABEE *runs up the stairs to the balcony.*)

MADGE. No, no, Jim!

LARRABEE. I tell you we will! Now's our chance to get hold of it! (LARRABEE *starts for* ALICE'S *door.* PRINCE *goes* U. S. *to the stairs and starts to go up stairs.*)

PRINCE. Well, I should say so!

(*THREE HEAVY KNOCKS are heard off* S. L. *Everyone stops. A sound of heavy blows as if struck from underneath the floor boards of the house. Beat.*)

LARRABEE. What's that?

MADGE. Someone at the door. (*She goes* S. R. C. *to the bell pull on the tower unit and pulls it.* PRINCE *crosses* D. S. L. *below the piano near the* U. S. *end of the desk.* FORMAN *enters from the door* U. L. C. *closing it behind*

him. He moves D. C. *to the edge of the platform* U. C.
and looks at MADGE. *All stand as if nothing has happened.*) I think someone knocked, Judson. (FORMAN
turns S. R. *and exits* U. R. *The sound of the front door
is heard closing.* FORMAN *comes back and stands to
the left of* MADGE.)

FORMAN. I beg pardon, ma'am, there's no one at the
door.

MADGE. That's all, Judson. (FORMAN *bows and exits*
U. L. C. *closing the door behind him.* PRINCE *moves to*
C. S. *as* LARRABEE *comes down the stairs and joins*
MADGE *and* PRINCE.)

PRINCE. 'E's got us watched! Wot we want to do is
to leave it alone and let the H'emperor have it!
(PRINCE *is holding his satchel and piece of pipe that
he was to use as a club on* HOLMES *if necessary.*)

MADGE. Do you mean Professor Moriarty?

PRINCE. That's 'oo I mean. Once let 'im get at it
and 'e'll settle it with 'Olmes pretty quick. Meet me
at Leary's nine sharp in the morning. Don't you worry!
I tell you the Professor will get 'im before tomorrow
night! 'E don't wait long either! And w'en he strikes,
it means death.

BLACKOUT

STREET SINGER *link going from* SCENE 1 *to* SCENE 2.

A STREET SINGER *enters from* D. S. L. *carrying a baby,
a bundle of bagged rags and a gin bottle. She goes*
C. S., *puts down the bundle of rags and sits on it.
As she starts to sing, an* INDIAN PRINCE *and an*
ESTATE AGENT *enter from* D. S. R., *cross to* L. C.
on the forestage. The INDIAN PRINCE *points out
building properties front as the* ESTATE AGENT
makes notes in his book.

STREET SINGER. (*Singing.*)
'TWAS IN THE MERRY MONTH OF MAY
WHEN MY TRUE LOVE I FIRST DID MEET
HE LOOKED JUST LIKE AN ANGEL BRIGHT
> (*She takes a drink of gin then gives some to the baby by putting it on her finger and then puts her finger to the baby's mouth. The* INDIAN PRINCE *and the* ESTATE AGENT *cross in front of her* S. L. *She mimes beggng for money as she continues to sing.*)

BUT HE DIED ALONE THERE IN THE
STREET
I LEFT THE TOWN ALL IN THE NIGHT
A WIDOW PLAGUED WITH WOE AND
STRIFE
BUT I WAS CHASED FROM LONDON TOWN
> (*The* INDIAN PRINCE *gives paper money to the* ESTATE AGENT, *then turns and exits* D. S. L. *The* ESTATE AGENT *pockets the money and tosses one coin onto the floor near the* STREET SINGER, *then he exits* D. S. L. *The* STREET SINGER *picks up the coin, bites it, then gets up, picking up her bundle and exits* D. S. L. *still singing.*)

FOR THEY DID SAY I TOOK HIS LIFE
> (TRUMPETER *joins in . . . from off* D. S. L. TRUMPETER *is* MORIARTY *theme as* VIOLIN *is* HOLMES.)

BUT JUSTICE FOLLOWED EVERY STEP
AND I WITH BITTERNESS DID CRY
FOR THE CRUEL JUDGE AND JURY
THEY BOTH CONDEMNED ME FOR TO DIE

ACT ONE

SCENE 2

This Scene is built inside the Second. PROFESSOR MORIARTY'S *underground office. A large vault-like room, with rough masonry walls and vaulted ceil-*

*ing. The general idea of this place is that it has
been converted from a cellar room of a warehouse
into a fairly comfortable office or headquarters.
There are no windows. The colour or tone of this
set must not be similar to the Second Act set,
which is a gloomy and dark bluish-brown. The
effect in this set should be of masonry that has
long ago been whitewashed and is now old,
stained and grimy. Maps on wall of England,
France, Germany, Russia, etc. Also a marked
map of London—heavy spots upon certain locali-
ties. Many charts of buildings, plans of floors—
possible tunnellings, etc.*

PROFESSOR JAMES MORIARTY *is seated at a large semi-
circular desk up* R. *facing the front. He is looking
over letters, telegrams, papers, etc. He is a middle-
aged man, with massive head and grey hair, and
a face full of character, overhanging brow, heavy
jaw . . . a man of great intellectual force, extremely tall and thin. His forehead domes out in
a white curve, and his two eyes are deeply sunken
in his head. Clean-shaven, pale, ascetic-looking.
Shoulders rounded and face protruding forward,
and forever oscillating from side to side in a
curiously reptilian fashion. Deep hollow voice.
The room is dark, with light showing on his face,
as if from a lamp. Pause. Once the revolve has
stopped in place and the lights have come up,*
JOHN *enters from* D. S. L. *and crosses to* MORIARTY
who is sitting at his desk C. S. R. *As* JOHN *reaches
the desk, he speaks.*

JOHN. Yes, sir?
MORIARTY. Has any report come in from Chibley?
JOHN. Nothing yet, sir.
MORIARTY. Send Bassick. (JOHN *turns and goes* S. L.
to the phone that hangs S. L. *of the door. He picks up
the receiver.*)

JOHN. John here. Send Bassick. (*He replaces the receiver on the hook and walks back to* MORIARTY'S *desk. As he reaches the desk, a BUZZER rings twice.* MORIARTY *picks up the tube* S. L. *side of the desk.*)

MORIARTY. Number. (*He puts the tube to his ear.*) Correct. (*He puts the cap back onto the tube as he replaces the tube in its socket; then he reaches for the lever* S. R. *to open the door. The MAGIC DOOR opens and* BASSICK *enters.* JOHN *exits immediately through the door as it closes behind him.* BASSICK *faces* MORIARTY. BASSICK *takes out his notebook and pencil.*) Before we go into anything else, I want to refer to Davidson.

BASSICK. I've made a note of him myself, sir; he's holding back money.

MORIARTY. Something like six hundred short on that last haul, isn't it?

BASSICK. Certainly as much as that.

MORIARTY. Have him attended to. Craigin is the one to do it. (BASSICK *writes a memo.*) And see that his disappearance is noticed. Have it spoken of. That finishes Davidson. Now, as to this Blaisdell matter, did you learn anything more?

BASSICK. The whole thing was a trap.

MORIARTY. What do you mean?

BASSICK. A trap set and baited by an expert.

MORIARTY. But those letters and papers of instructions, you brought them back, or destroyed them, I trust?

BASSICK. I could not do it, sir. Manning has disappeared and the papers are gone.

MORIARTY. Gone! Holmes again. That's bad for the Underwood trial.

BASSICK. But, I thought Shakleford was going to get a postponement.

MORIARTY. He tried to and found he was blocked.

BASSICK. Who could have done it? (MORIARTY *looks at* BASSICK.) Sherlock Holmes? (MORIARTY *overlaps* BASSICK'S *"Holmes."*)

MORIARTY. Holmes, Holmes, Holmes! He's got hold of thirty papers and instructions in as many different jobs, some as to putting a man or two out of the way. He's gradually completing chains of evidence which, if we let him go on will reach to me as surely as the sun will rise. Reach to me! He's playing rather a dangerous game! Inspector Wilson tried it seven years ago. Wilson is dead. Two years later Henderson took it up. We haven't heard anything of Henderson, lately, eh?

BASSICK. Not a thing, sir!

MORIARTY. This Holmes is rather a talented man. He hopes to drag me in at the Underwood trial, but he doesn't realize what can happen between now and Monday. There is not a street in London that will be safe for him if I whisper his name to Craigin. I might even make him a little call myself just for the satisfaction of it. Baker Street, isn't it? His place?

BASSICK. Baker Street, sir.

MORIARTY. We could make it absolutely secure for three streets each way?

BASSICK. Yes, sir, but . . .

MORIARTY. We could. We've done it elsewhere over and over again. Police decoyed. Men in every doorway. Do this tonight . . . in Baker Street! (BASSICK *takes notes.*) At nine o'clock call his attendants out on some pretext or other, and keep them out, you understand? I'll see this Sherlock Holmes myself. I'll give him a chance for his life. If he declines to treat with me . . . Holmes and I have been fencing for years. A hint there, a note here. The average inspector's only a generation away from a line of bumpkins stretching back into oblivion, but this . . . this Holmes . . . Over the years the pond gets smaller and smaller; we grow together like a couple of greedy old pike. Either I eat him or he eats me, or we choke on each other. But either way, one of us must go. They'll find his body washed up on the Isle of Dogs

and conclude it was a thick dark night that he slipped
on Waterloo Bridge with its low parapet. Once he's
dead they'll never find me; they'll never know.

(*The wall phone* S. L. *rings . . . one long count of six.*
BASSICK *puts his notebook and pencil away in his
vest pocket, left side.* MORIARTY *nods to* BASSICK
to attend to the phone. BASSICK *goes to the phone
that hangs* S. L. *of the door, picks it up and speaks
into the receiver.*)

BASSICK. Yes . . . yes . . . Bassick. What name
did you say? Prince yes. He'll have to wait. Yes, I
got his telegram last night. Well, tell him to come and
speak to me at the phone. Yes, I got your telegram,
Prince, but I have an important matter on. You'll
have to wait. Who? Sherlock Holmes? (MORIARTY
*picks up the receiver of his desk phone which is to his
left. He listens.*) Fighting against you in some job.
What sort of a game is it? Where is he now? Wait a
moment.

MORIARTY. Ask him what it is.

BASSICK. Prince . . .

MORIARTY. Wait! (*He puts the receiver down.*)
Send him here. (BASSICK *covers his receiver with his
hand.*)

BASSICK. No one sees you, sir. No one knows you.
That has meant safety for years.

MORIARTY. No one sees me now. You will talk with
him. I'll be there. This is *your office* . . . you understand . . . *your office*. I'll be there. (BASSICK *speaks
into his receiver.*)

BASSICK. Is that you, Prince? Yes, I find I can't
come out but I'll see you here. What interest have they
got? What's the name? (BASSICK *covers the receiver
with his hand and speaks to* MORIARTY.) He says
there's two with him . . . a man and a woman named
Larrabee. They won't consent to any interview unless
they're present.

MORIARTY. Send them in.

BASSICK. (*He speaks into the receiver.*) Prince? Ask John to come to the telephone. John those people with Prince, do they seem to be alright? Look close. Yes? Well, take them out through the warehouse and down by the circular stairway and then bring them here by the long tunnel. Yes, here! Look them over as you go along to see they're not carrying anything . . . and watch that no one sees you come down. Yes. (*He puts the receiver back onto the hook and looks at* MORIARTY.) I don't like this, sir.

MORIARTY. (*He stands at his desk.*) You lack stature, Bassick. (*The BUZZER rings two times.* MORIARTY *moves* S. R. *and gets onto the elevator.*) Your office, remember. Your office. (BASSICK *moves* S. C. R. *and gets behind the desk and sits in* MORIARTY'S *chair. He starts to reach for the lever that opens the door when the BUZZER rings three times.* BASSICK *picks up the tube, takes off the top and speaks into it.*)

BASSICK. Number. (*He listens then speaks into the tube.*) Are the three waiting with you? (*He listens then puts the tube back in its socket; then reaches for the lever to open the MAGIC DOOR.*)

(*The MAGIC DOOR swings open.* PRINCE *enters and crosses* S. R. *to the* S. R. *side of* MORIARTY'S *desk.* MADGE *enters and moves* D. S. L. *as* LARRABEE *enters and stands* D. S. R. *of the door; and* JOHN *enters and stands between* LARRABEE *and* MADGE *until* BASSICK *pushes the lever to close the MAGIC DOOR.* JOHN *then exits* D. S. L. *above* MADGE. MADGE *moves closer to* LARRABEE *as* JOHN *exits.*)

PRINCE. Morning, Alf.

BASSICK. I understand you to say, Prince, through our private telephone, that you've got something with Sherlock Holmes against you.

PRINCE. Yes, sir, we 'ave.

BASSICK. Kindly let me have the particulars.

PRINCE. Jim and Madge Larrabee here have picked up a girl in 'Omburg, where her sister had been havin' a strong affair of the heart with a very 'igh young foreign nob who promised to marry 'er . . . but the family stepped in and threw the whole thing down. 'E'd be'aved very bad to 'er, an had let 'imself out -an' written her letters, an' given her rings and tokens, yer see . . . and there was photographs too. Now, as these various things showed how 'e'd decieved and betrayed 'er, they wouldn't look very nice at all considerin' who the young man was, an' wot 'igh titles he was comin' into. So when this girl up and dies of it all, these letters and things all fall into the 'ands of the sister . . . which is the very one my friends Jim and Madge . . . Madge and Jim . . . 'ere has been nursin' all along.

BASSICK. Where have you kept her?

LARRABEE. We took a house up the Norrington Road.

BASSICK. How long have you been there?

LARRABEE. Two years, the fourteenth of next month.

BASSICK. And those letters and other evidences of the young man's misconduct, when will they reach their full value?

PRINCE. It's now, don't you see. It's now! There's a marriage comin' on an' there's been offers. The problem now is to get the papers in our hands.

BASSICK. Where are they?

PRINCE. Why, the girl's got 'old of 'em, sir!

LARRABEE. We had a safe for her to keep them in, supposing that when the time came we could open it, but the lock was out of order so we got Prince in to help us. He opened it last night and the package containing the things was gone . . .

BASSICK. What did you do when you discovered this?

PRINCE. Do . . . I hadn't any more than got the

safe open, sir, and' given one look at it, when Sherlock Holmes rings the front door bell.

BASSICK. There at your house?

LARRABEE. At my house.

BASSICK. *He didn't get those letters?*

LARRABEE. Well, he did get them, but he passed them back to the Faulkner girl. (*Bassick gets up from the desk and walks around* D. S. *in front of the desk toward* LARRABEE.)

BASSICK. Passed them back, eh? What did that mean?

LARRABEE. There's another thing that puzzles me. There was an accident below in the kitchen, a lamp fell off the table and scattered burning oil about, the butler ran up, yelling fire. We ran down there; and a few buckets of water put it out. (MORIARTY *moves to the elevator and steps onto it. He comes down to the Stage level and steps off the elevator.*)

MORIARTY. *I have a suggestion to make.* The first thing we must do is to get rid of your butler . . . not discharge him . . . get rid of him. (MORIARTY *goes behind his desk, sits and speaks to* BASSICK, *who jots down notes in his book* S. R. *of* MORIARTY'S *desk.*) Craigin for that! Today! As soon as it's dark. Give him two others to help; Mr. Larrabee will send the man into the cellar for something. They'll be waiting for him there. Doulton's van will get the body to the river. (MORIARTY *speaks to* MADGE.) It need not inconvenience you at all, Madam, we do these things very quietly. Bassick, what's the Seraph doing?

BASSICK. He's on the Reading job tomorrow night.

MORIARTY. Put him with Craigin today to help with that butler. But there's something else we want. (MORIARTY *turns to* LARRABEE *and* MADGE.) Have you seen those letters, the photographs, and whatever else there may be? Have you seen them? Do you know what they're like? (MADGE *steps* D. S. *and center to* MORIARTY.)

MADGE. I have. I've looked them through carefully several times. (BASSICK *stops taking notes.*)

MORIARTY. Could you make me a counterfeit set of those things and tie them up so that they will look exactly like the package Sherlock Holmes held in his hand last night?

MADGE. I could manage the letters but . . .

MORIARTY. If you manage the letters, I'll send some- -one who can manage the rest from your description. Bassick, that old German artist.

BASSICK. Leuftner.

MORIARTY. Precisely, Leuftner. Send Leuftner to Mrs. Larrabee at eleven. (MORIARTY *takes out his pocket watch with the left hand and puts it away.* BASSICK *takes notes.*) Quarter past ten. That gives you three quarters of an hour to reach home. I shall want that counterfeit package at eleven tonight. Twelve hours to make it.

MADGE. It will be ready, sir.

MORIARTY. Good! Bassick, notify the Lascar that I may require the Gas Chamber at Stepney tonight.

BASSICK. The Gas Chamber!

MORIARTY. Yes. The one that backs over the river . . . and have Craigin there a quarter before twelve with two others. Mr. Larrabee, I shall want you to write a letter to Mr. Sherlock Holmes which I shall dictate. And tonight, I may require a little assistance from you both. (BASSICK *stops taking notes.*) Meet me here at eleven.

LARRABEE. This is all very well, sir, but you have said nothing about the business arrangements. I'm not sure that I . . .

MORIARTY. You have no choice.

LARRABEE. No choice.

MORIARTY. No choice. I do as I please. It pleases me to take hold of this case.

LARRABEE. And what about pleasing me?

MORIARTY. I am not so sure but I shall be able to

do that as well. I will obtain the original letters from Miss Faulkner and negotiate them for much more than you could possibly obtain. In addition, you will have an opportunity tonight to sell the counterfeit package to Holmes for a good round sum. And the money obtained from both these sources shall be divided as follows: you will take one hundred per cent and I nothing.

LARRABEE. Nothing!

MORIARTY. Nothing!

BASSICK. But we cannot negotiate those letters until we know whom they incriminate. Mr. Larrabee has not yet informed us.

MORIARTY. Mr. Larrabee is wise in exercising caution. He values the keystone to his arch. But he will consent to let me know. (MADGE *moves to* MORIARTY'S *desk.*)

MADGE. Professor Moriarty, that information we would like to give only to you. (*She looks at* BASSICK. MORIARTY *motions* BASSICK *away.* BASSICK *moves* D. R. *and faces* U. S. *as he puts his notebook and pencil into his pocket.* PRINCE *also faces* U. S. MORIARTY *tears off a piece of paper from the pad in front of him and pushes it toward* MADGE; *then takes the pencil and slides it in her direction. She takes the pencil and writes a name, puts the pencil down and pushes the note toward* MORIARTY. *PAUSE.* MORIARTY *looks at the piece of paper which he moves in front of himself. PAUSE.*)

MORIARTY. This is an absolute certainty.

LARRABEE. Absolute.

MORIARTY. It means you have a fortune. Had I known this, you should hardly have had such terms.

LARRABEE. Oh well, we don't object to a . . .

MORIARTY. The arrangement is made Mr. Larrabee. I bid you good morning. (LARRABEE *moves* D. S. L. *as* MORIARTY *stands offering his hand to* MADGE. *She takes his hand curtsies to him. He lets go of her hand, sits and reaches for the lever for the door. He pulls the lever toward him and the door opens.* PRINCE *crosses* S. L. *and exits followed by* MADGE *and* LARRABEE. BAS-SICK *starts to exit* S. L. *just as* MORIARTY *pushes the lever to close the door which shuts in* BASSICK'S *face. PAUSE.* BASSICK *turns to* MORIARTY *for instructions.*) Bassick place your men at nine tonight for Sherlock Holmes' house in Baker Street.

BASSICK. You will go there *yourself*, sir?

MORIARTY. I will go there *myself . . . myself.* I will offer him peace or . . . (MORIARTY *opens the* S. R. *top drawer of his desk and takes out a revolver.*) death.

BASSICK. But this meeting tonight at twelve to trap Holmes in the Gas Chamber in Swandem Lane.

MORIARTY. If I fail in Baker Street, (MORIARTY *takes the note* MADGE *had handed him, strikes a match and lites the note and watches it burn.*) we'll trap him tonight in Swandem Lane. Either way I have him, I have him. (MORIARTY *drops the burning note into a brass bowl in front of him and puts his hand over the bowl.*)

BLACKOUT

Link Scene going from SCENE 2 *to* SCENE 3.

The PENNY WHISTLE PLAYER *enters from the pit* S. R., *moves onto the forestage, stands and plays the penny whistle* D. S. R. JOHN, *dressed as a policeman, enters from* D. S. L., *crosses to* C. S. *and faces* U. S. *PAUSE.* JOHN *turns to the* PENNY WHISTLE PLAYER.

JOHN. Come along now, come along. Try the Oxford Street pitch.

(*The* PENNY WHISTLE PLAYER *stops playing, crosses
to* D. S. L., *moving in front of* JOHN, *turns back
to face* JOHN *and blows a screeching note, i.e., "up
yours," on the penny whistle, then exits* D. S. L.
JOHN *is standing* D. S. C. R. *when* BASSICK *enters
dressed as an inspector. He is followed by a*
TRUMPETER. BASSICK *moves to the* S. L. *side of*
JOHN *by going* U. S. *of* JOHN. *The* TRUMPETER
remains U. S. R. *of them.*)

BASSICK. All clear now in Baker Street, Constable?
JOHN. All clear now, Inspector Bassick. (*Laughs
at his own joke.*)
BASSICK. Sssssh!

(BASSICK *turns to the* TRUMPETER *who moves* D. S. *and
signals him to start playing. The* TRUMPETER
plays. JOHN *and* BASSICK *turn and exit* D. S. L.
As the TRUMPETER *repeats a phrase, he turns and
exits* D. S. R. *still playing the trumpet as the SET
REVOLVES into BAKER STREET with* SHER-
LOCK HOLMES *sitting in front of the fireplace
playing his violin by fire light.*)

ACT ONE

SCENE 3

In SHERLOCK HOLMES' *rooms in Baker Street—the
large drawing room of his apartments. An open,
cheerful room, but not too much decorated.
Rather plain. The walls are a plain tint, the ceil-
ing ditto. The furniture is comfortable and good,
but not elegant. Books, music, violins, tobacco
pouches, pipes, tobacco, etc. are scattered in
places about the room with some disorder. Various
odd things are hung about. Some very choice pictures and etchings hang on the walls here and*

*there, but the pictures do not have heavy gilt
frames. All rather simple. The room gives more
an impression of an artist's studio. A fireplace
U. C. with a cheerful grate fire burning, throwing
a red glow into room. A laboratory with a table
of chemicals and various knick-knacks S. R. Furniture according to the Scene plot. The lighting
should be arranged so that after the dark change
the first thing that becomes visible—even before
the rest of the room—is the glow of the fire, the
blue flame of the spirit lamp—and* SHERLOCK
HOLMES *seated among cushions on the floor before
the fire. Light gradually on, but still leaving the
effect of only firelight. Music stops, just as
LIGHTS UP.*

SHERLOCK HOLMES' *is discovered on the floor before the
fire. He is in a dressing gown and slippers and has
his pipe. He is playing a violin. Once* HOLMES
*finishes playing the violin, he puts the bow down
to his right . . . BEAT . . . then he puts down
the violin into its case with the bow. He picks up
his pipe and puts it in his mouth. As he takes
the pipe out of his mouth,* HOLMES *puts his pipe
down on the S. R. side of the mantle near the pipe
rack. He then turns back S. L. to watch as* BILLY
opens the door and enters.

BILLY. It's Doctor Watson, sir. You told me as I
could always show him up.

HOLMES. Well, I should think so. (DOCTOR WATSON
enters and BILLY *exits closing the door.*) Watson, my
dear fellow. (HOLMES *goes to him and they shake
hands.*)

WATSON. How are you, Holmes?

HOLMES. Perfectly delighted to see you, (HOLMES
*crosses U. L. to the sidetable to get the brandy de-
canteur and brandy glass then crosses D. C. L. to put*

them on the table as WATSON *takes off his coat and hangs it up on the coat/hat rack that is on the door. He puts his hat on the* S. L. *side of the table.*) my dear fellow, perfectly delighted. Wedlock suits you, Watson. (HOLMES *stands at the* U. S. R. *end of the table looking at* WATSON.) You have put on seven and one half pounds since I saw you.

WATSON. Seven actually.

HOLMES. (*He turns* U. S. L. *and goes* U. L. *to the coal tin that is* S. L. *of the fireplace. The cigar box is placed in the coal tin.* HOLMES *picks up the cigar box.*) Indeed I should have thought a little more. Just a trifle more I fancy. (HOLMES *moves* D. C. L. *and puts the cigar box on the* S. R. *side of the table.*) But I also infer that you are in danger of losing it again if your wife remains away from home much longer. (WATSON *pours himself a brandy.*)

WATSON. Indeed she returns tomorrow from a little visit. (WATSON *takes a cigar from the cigar box.*) But how do you know? (HOLMES *puts his hands in the pockets of his dressing gown.*)

HOLMES. How did I know? I observed it. How do I know that you have opened a consulting room and resumed the practice of medicine without letting me hear a word about it? How do I know that you've been getting yourself very wet lately, that you have a most clumsy and careless servant girl and that you've moved your dressing table to the other side of your room? (HOLMES *turns and goes* U. C. *to the mantle to pick up the syringe case then crosses* D. C. L. *and puts the case on top of the cigar box on the table.* WATSON *crosses* S. R. *to the* D. R. *chair and sits holding his brandy glass.*)

WATSON. My dear Holmes, if you lived a few centuries ago, they would certainly have burned you alive.

HOLMES. (*He puts his left hand on the back of the chair* S. R. *of the table.*) Whereas you, my dear Doctor, would be as safe as houses in any century you chose. (HOLMES *crosses* C. S. *and faces front.*) Lucky man.

WASTON. Tell me, how did you know all that?

HOLMES. It is simplicity itself. There are scratches and parallel cuts on your right boot, there where the firelight strikes it. Somebody scraped away crusted mud and did it badly. There's your wet feet and careless servant girl all on one boot. (HOLMES *moves* C. S. R. *toward* WATSON.) Face badly shaved on your right side, used to be your left . . . couldnt' well move your window . . . must have moved your dressing table. (HOLMES *touches* WATSON's *cheek as he moves* S. R. *to the chemistry table to pick up phile to fill the syringe.*)

WASTON. Yes, by Jove! But my medical practice, I fail to see how you worked that out.

HOLMES. (*He moves* C. S. *going toward the table then stops and turns to* WATSON.) My dear Watson, if a gentleman walks into my room reeking of iodoform, and with a black mark of nitrate on the inside of his right forefinger, the characteristic tiny bulge in his hat where he normally secretes his stethescope, I must be dull indeed if I do not pronounce him to be an active member of the medical profession. (HOLMES *moves to the table and opens the syringe case.*)

WATSON. Ha! Ha! Of course. (HOLMES *puts the needle on the syringe.*) But how the deuce did you know that my wife was away and . . .

HOLMES. (*He looks up as he fills the syringe.*) Where the deuce is your second waistcoat button, and what the deuce is yesterday's caranation doing in today's lapel? Oh, this is elementary, my dear Watson. Child's play of deduction. (*He puts the syringe in his mouth while he rolls up his left sleeve. He gives himself an injection, puts the needle back into its case and then rubs his arm.* WATSON *stands and moves* C. S. *holding his brandy and watching* HOLMES.)

WATSON. Which is it today? Cocaine or morphine or . . .

HOLMES. Cocaine, my dear fellow. (HOLMES *still rubbing his arm.*) A seven per cent solution. (HOLMES

stops rubbing his arm.) I'm back to my old love.
(*Offers syringe to* WATSON.) Would you like to try
some?

WATSON. (*He turns away and moves* S. R.) Certainly
not.

HOLMES. (*He picks up the syringe case and moves*
U. C. *to put it back onto the mantle then turns and
moves* D. C.) Oh! I'm so sorry!

WATSON. I have no wish to break *my* system down
before it's time. (*He finishes his brandy.* HOLMES
points to WATSON *with the syringe.*)

HOLMES. Quite right, my dear Doctor, quite right,
but, (HOLMES. *goes to the mantle and puts the syringe
case down on it.*) you see, my time has come. (HOLMES
moves D. S. *to the* S. R. *side of the fireplace where he
was playing the violin sitting on the pillows and throws
himself back onto the pillows . . . ends up sitting
with his arms folded in front of him.* WATSON *moves*
U. R. C. *and sits on the edge of the fire fender behind*
HOLMES *holding his brandy glass.*)

WATSON. Holmes, for months I have seen you using
these deadly drugs in ever increasing doses. When they
lay hold of you there is no end. It must go on and on
until the finish.

HOLMES. So must you go on and on, eating your
breakfast until the finish.

WATSON. Breakfast is food. These drugs are poisons
. . . slow but certain. They involve tissue changes of
a most *serious* nature.

HOLMES. Just what I want. I'm bored to death with
my old tissues. I want to get a whole new lot.

WATSON. (*He puts his left hand on* HOLMES' *right
shoulder.*) Ah, really, Holmes, I'm trying to save you.

HOLMES. (*He puts his left hand on* WATSON'S.)
You can't do it, old fellow, so don't waste your time.
(WATSON *takes his hand off* HOLMES' *shoulder. He
stands and moves* D. C. L. *to the table and sits in the
U. C. chair at the table. PAUSE.*) Watson, to change

the subject a little. (WATSON *pours another brandy.*) In the enthusiasm which has prompted you to chronicle and if you will excuse my saying so, somewhat to embellish a few of my little adventures, you have occasionally committed the error or indiscretion of giving them a certain tinge of romance (WATSON *takes out a cigar and shifts around in his chair more toward* HOLMES.) which struck me as being a trifle out of place. Something like working an elopement into the fifth proposition of Euclid. (WATSON *lights his cigar from matches he carries in his pocket.*) I merely refer to this in case you should see fit at some future time to chronicle the most important and far-reaching case in my career . . . one upon which I have labored for nearly fourteen months, and which is now rapidly approaching (HOLMES *looks quickly at the clock on the mantle.*) a singularly diverting climax. I allude to the case of Professor James Moriarty. (WATSON *shifts his chair more* C. S. *to face* HOLMES. WATSON *leans forward with his elbows resting on his knees.*)

WATSON. Moriarty! I don't remember ever having heard of the fellow.

HOLMES. (*He sits up facing front with his hands clasped on his knees.*) The Napoleon of crime. The Napoleon! He sits motionless like an ugly venomous spider in the center of his web . . . (HOLMES *looks to* WATSON.) but that web has ten thousand radiations and that spider (HOLMES *faces front moving his left hand is a quivering like motion in front of him going from* S. L. *to* S. R.) knows every quiver of every one of them.

WATSON. Really! This is very interesting. (HOLMES *turns to* WATSON *with his hands on his knees.*)

HOLMES. Ah, but, my dear Doctor, the real interest will come when the Professor begins to realize his position which he cannot fail to do shortly. By ten o'clock tomorrow night the time will be ripe for the arrests. Then the greatest criminal trial of the century . . .

the clearing up of over forty mysteries and the rope for everyone. (WATSON *slaps his thigh with his left hand then points to* HOLMES.)

WATSON. Good! But what will he do when he sees that you have him?

HOLMES. Do? (HOLMES *faces front.*) He will do me the honor, (HOLMES *leans back onto the pillows with his arms resting behind his head.*) my dear Watson, of bending every resource of his wonderful organization of criminals to the one purpose of my destruction.

WATSON. (*He puts his brandy glass down onto the table and stands and moves* U. S. C. *toward the fireplace.*) Why, Holmes, this is a *dangerous* thing.

HOLMES. On the contrary, it's perfectly delightful! It saves me any number of doses of those deadly drugs upon which you occasionally favor me with your medical views! (WATSON *takes a puff on his cigar.*) Watson, my whole life is spent in a series of frantic endeavors to escape from the dreary common-place of existence! For a brief period I escape! You should congratulate me!

WATSON. But you could escape them without such serious risks! Your other cases have not been so dangerous, and they were even more interesting. (HOLMES *sits up.*) Now, the one you spoke of the last time I saw you . . . the recovery of those damaging letters and gifts from a young girl who . . . (HOLMES *picks up the violin and holds it upside down then turns it sideways in front of him.*) A most peculiar affair as I remember it. (HOLMES *picks up the bow.*) You were going to try the experiment of making her betray their hiding place by an alarm of fire in her own home and after that . . . (HOLMES *rubs the bow over the strings.*)

HOLMES. Precisely, after that.

WATSON. Didn't the plan succeed?

HOLMES. Of course, as far as I've gone.

WATSON. You got Forman into the house as butler?

HOLMES. (*He rubs the bow over the strings again.*) Forman was in as butler.

WATSON. And upon your signal he overturned a lamp in the kitchen, scattered the smoke balls and gave an alarm of fire? (HOLMES *rubs the bow over the strings.*) And the young lady, did she . . . (HOLMES *stops rubbing the bow over the strings and puts the violin and bow back into the case.* HOLMES *gets up and moves* D. S. R. *between the footstool and* D. R. *chair.*)

HOLMES. Yes, she did, Watson. She did. (WATSON *puts his cigar in his mouth.*) It all transpired precisely as planned. I took the package of papers from its hiding place and as I told you I would, I handed it back to Miss Faulkner. (WATSON *takes the cigar out of his mouth as he moves* D. S. C. *on a level with* HOLMES.)

WASTON. But you never told me *why* you proposed to hand it back.

HOLMES. For a very simple reason, my dear Watson. That it would have been theft for me to take it. The contents of the package were the absolute property of the young lady.

WATSON. Yes, but what did you *gain* by this?

HOLMES. Her confidence, and so far as I was able to secure it, her regard. (HOLMES *pulls down his left shirt sleeve and re-fastens the cuff link.*) As it was impossible for me to take possession of the letters, photographs and jewelry in that package without her consent, my only alternative is to obtain that consent . . . to induce her to give it to me of her own free will. (HOLMES *sits in the* D. R. *chair putting his feet up on the footstool.*) Its return to her after I had laid hands on it was the first move in that direction. The second will depend entirely upon what transpires today. I expect Forman here to report in half an hour. (*The door* S. L. *opens and* TERESE *enters closing the door behind her.* HOLMES *stands up.*)

TERESE. I beg you to pardon me, sir. (HOLMES *moves to her* S. L. *above the table.*) Ze boy he say to come right up as soon as I come. (HOLMES *takes her* C. S. *as he moves* D. S. R. *near the footstool.*)

HOLMES. Quite right! Quite right!

TERESE. Ah! I fear me zere is trouble, M'sieur. Ze butlair, your assestant, ze one who sent me to you . . .

HOLMES. Forman?

TERESE. Heem! Forman! Zere eez somesing done to heem! I fear to go down to see.

HOLMES. Down where?

TERESE. Ze down. Ze cellaire of zat house. Eet ees a dreadful place. He deed not come back. He went down . . . he deed not come up.

(*BEAT.* HOLMES *runs* S. L. *to the table and picks up the hand bell and rings it then moves* U. L. *to the sidetable and opens the* U. S. *drawer and loads his gun and slips it into his left hand pocket of his dressing gown.* WATSON *watches all this from* U. C. *putting his cigar in his mouth.*)

HOLMES. Who sent him down?

TERESE. M'sieur of ze house, M'sieur Chetwood.

HOLMES. Larrabee.

TERESE. Oui.

HOLMES. Has he been down there long?

TERESE. No, for I soon suspect ze dreadful noise was heard. Oh, ze noise! Ze noise!

HOLMES. (*He is still loading his gun.*) What noise?

TERESE. Ze noise! (HOLMES *moves down to her putting his arm around her as he quickly moves her to the* D. R. *chair and sits her in it. He then moves* C. S.)

HOLMES. Try to be calm and answer me. What did it sound like? (WATSON *takes his cigar out of his mouth.* HOLMES *moves back* U. L. *to the sidetable and loads another gun which he'll give to* WATSON.)

TERESE. Ze dreadful cry of a man who eeze struck down by some deadly seeng. (BILLY *enters* S. L. *and closes the door behind him.*)

HOLMES. Coat, boot, and order a cab. Quick! (BILLY *runs* U. R., *opens the side door, gets* HOLMES' *coat, closes the door, runs* D. R. *and throws the coat over the back of the* D. R. *chair and runs* S. L. *to the door.*)

BILLY. Yes, sir.

HOLMES. Did anyone follow him down?

TERESE. I did not see.

HOLMES. Don't wait. Order the cab. (BILLY *exits out the* S. L. *door closing it behind him.* HOLMES *turns to* WATSON.) The game's afoot, Watson. (HOLMES *hands* WATSON *a revolver.*) Take this and follow me.

TERESE. (*She stands up.*) I had not better go also?

HOLMES. No. (HOLMES *moves* C. S. *toward* TERESE.) Wait here! Ah! I hear Forman coming now.

(WATSON *moves* D. L. *and puts his cigar out in the ashtray on the table.* FORMAN'S *footsteps are heard running toward the* S. L. *door.* WATSON *turns to the* S. L. *door and opens it just in time for* FORMAN *to stumble in and leans on the* U. C. *chair trying to catch his breath.* WATSON *puts the revolver in his right pocket.*)

FORMAN. Nothing more last night, sir. After you left, Prince came in, and they made a start for her room to get the package away, but I gave the three knocks with an axe on the floor beams as you directed, and they didn't get any farther. But then this morning, a little after nine . . .

HOLMES. (*He turns to* TERESE.) One moment.

FORMAN. Yes, sir?

HOLMES. Mademoiselle, step into that room and rest yourself. (*He indicated the door* U. R.)

TERESE. I am not tired, Monsieur.

HOLMES. (*He moves* U. R. *to the door.*) Then step

into that room and walk about a bit. I'll let you know
when you are required.

TERESE. Oui, Monsieur. (*She exits* U. R. *and* HOLMES
*closes the door behind her and removes the key in the
lock putting it on the* S. R. *end of the mantle.* FORMAN
sits in the U. C. *chair at the table.*)

HOLMES. Take a look at his head, Watson.

FORMAN. It's nothing at all.

HOLMES. Take a look at his head, Watson.

WATSON. (*He examines* FORMAN'S *head.*) An ugly
bruise but not dangerous. (WATSON *moves* U. L. C. *and
sits on the edge of the side table as* HOLMES *comes*
D. C. *toward* FORMAN.)

HOLMES. Very well. At a little after nine, you
say . . .

FORMAN. Yes, sir. (HOLMES *turns and goes to the*
D. R. *chair and sits with his hands on his knees.*) This
morning a little after nine, Larrabee and his wife drove
away and she returned about eleven without him. A
little later, old Leuftner came and the two went to
work in the library. (FORMAN *gets up and moves* S. R.
toward HOLMES.) I got a look at them from the outside
and found they were making up a *counterfeit of the
package we are working for!* You'll have to watch for
some sharp trick, sir. (WATSON *stands and moves down
to the* U. C. *chair at the table.*)

HOLMES. No, *they'll* have to watch for the sharp
trick, Forman! And Larrabee, what of him?

FORMAN. He came back a little after three.

HOLMES. How did he seem?

FORMAN. Under great excitement, sir.

HOLMES. Any marked resentment towards you?

FORMAN. I think there was, sir, though he tried not
to show it.

HOLMES. He has consulted someone outside. Was the
Larrabee woman's behavior different also?

FORMAN. She gave me an ugly look as she came in.

HOLMES. (*He leans back in his chair with one foot on the footstool.*) Ah, an ugly look. She was present at the consultation. They were advised to get rid of you. He sent you down into the cellar on some pretext. (*He sits up straight.*) You were attacked in the dark by two men . . . possibly three . . . (HOLMES *gets up and moves* C. S. *toward* FORMAN.) and received a bad blow from a sand club. You managed to strike down one of your assailants with a stone . . . (HOLMES *grabs* FORMAN's *right hand, looks at it and lets it go.*) no, a piece of timber and escaped from the others in the dark, crawling out through a coal grating.

FORMAN. That's what took place, sir.

HOLMES. They have taken in a partner, and a dangerous one at that. He not only directed this conspiracy against you, but he also advised the making of the counterfeit package. (HOLMES *returns to the* D. R. *chair and sits in it leaning back and putting both feet on the footstool.*) Within a very short time I shall receive an offer from Mr. Larrabee to sell me the package. He will indicate that Miss Faulkner has changed her mind and has concluded to get what she can for them. He will desire to meet me on the subject and will then endeavor to sell me his bogus package for an enormous sum of money. After that . . . (HOLMES *puts his left hand out as if to receive a letter at the exact moment* BILLY *comes in the* S. L. *door and runs to* HOLMES *with a letter.*)

BILLY. Letter, sir! Most important letter, sir! (BILLY *puts the letter in* HOLMES' *hand.*)

HOLMES. Unless I am greatly mistaken . . . (HOLMES *takes the envelop and rubs it across his forehead with his left hand.*) the said communication is at hand. It is. (HOLMES *gives the letter back to* BILLY *who crosses* S. L. *to hand it to* WATSON. WATSON *takes it and sits in the* U. C. *chair.*) Read it for me Watson, there's a good fellow. My eyes, you know, cocaine . . . and all those things you like so much. (WATSON *opens the letter and reads as* FORMAN *moves behind him and* BILLY *stand* U. S. *of him looking over his shoulder.*)

WATSON. "Dear Sir."

HOLMES. Who thus addresses me? (HOLMES *puts his right hand onto his forehead.* WATSON *turns the letter over to look at the signature.*)

WATSON. "James Larrabee."

HOLMES. What a surprise! And what has James to say this evening?

WATSON. "Dear Sir."

HOLMES. I do hope he won't say that again.

WATSON. "I have the honor to inform you that Miss Faulkner has changed her mind regarding the letters, etc., (HOLMES *drops his hand from his forehead and lets it drop over the* D. S. *arm of the chair.*) which you wish to obtain, and has decided to dispose of them for a monetary consideration. She has placed them in my hands for this purpose, and if you are in a position to offer a good round sum, and to pay it down at once in cash, the entire lot is yours. (HOLMES *takes out his note pad and pencil from the right hand pocket of his dressing gown and jots down a note.*) If you wish to negotiate, however, it must be tonight, at the house of a friend of mine, in the city. (HOLMES *closes his note pad, folds the note he has torn off and crosses his right leg over his left.*) At eleven o'clock you will be at the Guards' Monument at the foot of Waterloo Place. You will see a cab with wooden shutters to the windows. Enter it (WATSON *turns the letter over.*) and the driver will bring you to my friend's house. If you have the cab followed, or try any other underhand trick, you won't get what you want. Let me know your decision. Yours truly, James Larrabee."

HOLMES. Now let me see if I have the points. Tonight, eleven o'clock, Guards' Monument, Waterloo Place, cab with wooden shutters. No one to accompany me. No one to follow cab or I don't get what I want.

WATSON. Quite right. (HOLMES *puts the note pad and pencil back into his right hand pocket.*)

HOLMES. Ah!

WATSON. But this cab with the wooden shutters.

HOLMES. A simple device to keep me from seeing where I am driven. Billy! (BILLY *crosses* S. R. *to* HOLMES.)

BILLY. Yes, sir. (HOLMES *sits up putting his elbows on his knees.* FORMAN *moves* U. C.)

HOLMES. Who brought it?

BILLY. It was a woman, sir.

HOLMES. Ah, old or young?

BILLY. Werry old, sir.

HOLMES. In a cab?

BILLY. Yes, sir.

HOLMES. Seen the driver before?

BILLY. Yes, sir . . . but I can't think where. (HOLMES *leans back in the chair crossing his left leg over his right and hands* BILLY *the note.*)

HOLMES. Very well. Hand this to the old lady. Apologize for the delay, and take a good look at that driver again.

BILLY. (*He runs* S. L. *and out the door.*) Yes, sir. (WATSON *stands and moves* C. S. *toward* HOLMES *crossing in front of* FORMAN.)

WATSON. My dear Holmes, you did not say you would go?

HOLMES. Certainly I did.

WATSON. But it is the counterfeit.

HOLMES. The counterfeit is exactly what I want.

WATSON. Why so?

HOLMES. Because with it I shall obtain the original. (HOLMES *gets up and moves* U. R. *to the door and opens it.*) Mademoiselle!

WATSON. (*He crosses back to the* U. C. *chair at the table and sits.*) But this fellow means mischief.

(HOLMES *turns to* WATSON *and moves* C. S. *as* TERESE
*comes out and closes the door behind her. She
moves down to* HOLMES' *right side.*)

HOLMES. This fellow means the same. Be so good,
Mademoiselle, as to listen to every word. Tonight at
twelve o'clock I meet Mr. Larrabee and purchase from
him the false bundle of letters to which you just now
heard us refer, as you were listening at the keyhole of
that door.

TERESE. Oui, Monsieur.

HOLMES. I wish Miss Faulkner to know *at once*
that I propose to buy this package tonight.

TERESE. I will tell her, Monsieur.

HOLMES. That is my wish. But do not tell her that
I know this package and its contents to be counterfeit.
She is to suppose that I think I am buying the
genuine. (HOLMES *moves slightly away from* TERESE
going S. L. C.)

TERESE. Oui, Monsieur, je comprends. When you
purchase you think you have the *real*. (HOLMES *goes
to her and helps her to the door* S. L.)

HOLMES. Precisely. One thing more. Tomorrow evening I shall want you to accompany her to this place,
here. Sir Edward Leighton and Count Von Stalburg
will be here to receive the package at my hands. But,
you will receive further instructions as to this in the
morning. (HOLMES *opens the door to let her out.* TERESE
crosses in front of him and goes out the door which
HOLMES *closes.*)

TERESE. Oui, Monsieur.

HOLMES. Forman.

FORMAN. Yes, sir?

HOLMES. Change to your beggar disguise Number
14, and go (HOLMES *crosses* S. R. C.) through every
den in Limehouse and Wapping. Don't stop till you
get a clue to this new partner of the Larrabees. I must
have that. I must have that.

FORMAN. (*He starts to go* S. L. *to the door.*) Very well, sir. (BILLY *enters the* S. L. *door and closes it behind him.*)

BILLY. If you please, sir, there's a man awaitin' at the street door and 'e says 'e must speak to Mr. Forman, sir, as quick as 'e can.

HOLMES. (*He turns and moves* U. C.) We'd better have a look at that man. Billy, show him up.

BILLY. 'E can't come up, sir . . . 'e's a-watchin' a man in the street. 'E says 'e's from Scotland Yard. (HOLMES *turns and moves* R. C. *as* FORMAN *goes to the* S. L. *door and opens it.*)

FORMAN. I'd better see what it is, sir. (*He exits closing the door behind him. BEAT.*)

HOLMES. NO! (FORMAN *quickly re-enters holding the door ajar waiting for instructions.*) Well, take a look at him first. *Be ready for anything.* (HOLMES *paces* U. L. *and then* D. C.)

FORMAN. Trust me for that, sir. (FORMAN *exits closing the door behind him.*)

HOLMES. See what he does, Billy.

BILLY. Yes, sir. (BILLY *exits closing the door behind him.* HOLMES *runs* U. S. R. *to the circular staircase. He goes up the staircase and crosses* S. L. *on the balcony to the draped window and peers out between the drapes on the* U. S. L. *wall.*)

WATSON. This is becoming interesting. Look here, Holmes, you've given me a halfway look into this case . . .

HOLMES. (*He continues to look out the window.*) What case?

WATSON. (*Re-reading letter to check the name.*) This strange case of . . . Miss . . .

HOLMES. Quite so. One moment, my dear fellow. Ring the bell, Watson. (WASTON *reaches for the hand bell and rings it. PAUSE.* BILLY *enters the* S. L. *door and closes it behind him.* BILLY *looks at* DR. WATSON *who indicates to him that* HOLMES *is up on the bal-*

cony. HOLMES *closes the drape and leans on the balcony rail looking down to* BILLY.) Mr. Forman, is he there still?

BILLY. No, sir, 'e's gone. (*Pause.*)

HOLMES. That's all. (*He looks out the drapes again.*)

BILLY. Thank you, sir. (*He exits* S. L. *closing the door behind him.* HOLMES *crosses* S. R. *on the balcony to the stairs.*)

HOLMES. As you were saying, Watson. This strange case of . . . (HOLMES *stops for a moment on the second and third steps down on the staircase.* WATSON *looks at the letter to check the name.*)

WATSON. Of Miss Faulkner.

HOLMES. Precisely. This strange case of Miss Faulkner (HOLMES *comes down the stairs and crosses* U. C. *to the mantle.*)

WATSON. You've given me some idea of it. Now don't you think it would be only fair to let me have the rest?

HOLMES. (*He picks up the Persian slipper filled with tobacco on the* S. R. *side of the mantle along with his pipe.*) What shall I tell you? (HOLMES *moves* D. C. *opening the Persian slipper and filling his pipe.*)

WATSON. You could tell me what you propose to do with that counterfeit package which you are going *to risk your life to obtain.*

HOLMES. Oh, my life is worth nothing when it defends so heroic a purpose! I shall assist a man who has robbed a young girl of life and honor to rob her sister of her property. I intend, with the aid of the counterfeit, to make her willingly hand me the genuine. I shall accomplish this by a piece of trickery and deceit of which I am heartily ashamed (HOLMES *faces front.*) and which I would never have undertaken if I had known her as I do now. It's too bad, Watson. She's rather a nice girl.

WATSON. Nice girl, is she? Then you think that possibly . . .

BILLY. (*He enters quickly at the* S. L. *door and closes it behind him.*) I beg pardon, sir, Mr. Forman's just sent out from the chemist's on the corner to say his head is a-paining 'im a bit, an' would Dr. Watson kindly step over and get 'im something to put on it. (HOLMES *goes* S. R. *to the chemistry counter and checks the liquid in one of the tubes.* WATSON *takes a last sip of his brandy and puts the glass down on the table as he stands up.* BILLY *gets* WATSON's *coat from the coat rack on the door and picks up his hat from the* S. L. *side of the table.*)

WATSON. Yes, certainly, I'll go at once. That's singular. It didn't look like anything serious. I'll be back in a minute, Holmes. (BILLY *hands* WATSON *his coat and hat and holds the door open for him.* WATSON *exits and* BILLY *closes the door.* HOLMES *crosses* C. S. BILLY *moves* C. S. *toward* HOLMES.)

HOLMES. Billy. Who brought that message from Forman?

BILLY. Boy from the chemist's, sir.

HOLMES. Yes, of course, but which boy?

BILLY. I couldn't see clearly, he stood a few yards off in the fog, but I'm sure I ain't seen him before. He was very big for a chemist's boy.

HOLMES. (*He is still holding his pipe and the Persian slipper.*) Quick, Billy, run down and look after the doctor. If the boy's gone and there's a man with him it means mischief. Let me know quick. Don't stop to come up, ring the door bell. I'll hear it. Ring it loud. Quick now.

(BILLY *runs out the* S. L. *door closing it behind him.* HOLMES *puts his pipe in his mouth and tosses the Persian slipper onto the mantle* U. C. *He stops and listens for a moment then goes* D. C. L. *and arranges the chair that is* S. R. *of the table.* MORI- ARTY *will sit in this chair.* HOLMES *goes* U. L. *to the sidetable and turns off the lamp that is on the* U. S. *end of the sidetable. He goes to the mantle to pick up a box of matches and walks slowly* D. S. C. *taking out a match from the match box. He strikes the match on the side of the match box and starts to light his pipe. THE DOOR BELL RINGS.* HOLMES *stops and holds the burning match. PAUSE.*)

BILLY. (*Off* S. L.) Sir! Sir!

(HOLMES *tosses the match* S. R. *and the match box* U. C. *onto the mantle. He goes to the* D. R. *chair and sits, leaning back 'with his feet on the foot stool. He puts his right hand which is holding the pipe into his dressing gown pocket to give the impression of holding a gun. He waits looking at the* S. L. *door. The door swings open and* MORIARTY *steps in. The door swings back past* MORIARTY *who reaches behind him and grabs the door knob and closes the door.* MORIARTY *walks slowly to* C. S. *keeping his right hand behind him as he observes* HOLMES. HOLMES *slightly lifts his right hand in his dressing gown pocket.*)

MORIARTY. A dangerous habit to finger loaded firearms in the pocket of one's dressing down.

HOLMES. You will go straight from here to the hospital if you keep that hand behind you. (MORIARTY *slowly exposes his right hand from behind his back. His hand is empty.*)

MORIARTY. You evidently do not know me.

HOLMES. (*He stands up taking the pipe out of his right pocket.*) On the contrary, I think it is fairly evident that I do. (*He puts the pipe in his mouth.*) I can spare you five minutes if you have anything to say. (MORIARTY *moves his right hand as if to take something from inside his coat pocket.* HOLMES *quickly takes out his revolver from his left hand pocket and*

holds it pointed at MORIARTY.) What were you about
to do?

MORIARTY. Look at my watch. (HOLMES *crosses* S. L.
above MORIARTY *going above the table to the* S. L.
chair at the table all the while holding the revolver on
MORIARTY.)

HOLMES. I'll tell you when the five minutes is up.
(HOLMES *adjusts his chair to the table and points to
the* S. R. *chair at the table for* MORIARTY *to sit.*) Pray
take a chair. (MORIARTY *puts his hat and cane down
on the* S. R. *side of the table then starts to sit in the
chair* S. R. *of the table at the same moment* HOLMES
starts to sit at the S. L. *side of the table. Both stop
and check each other then they both sit.* HOLMES *puts
his gun down on the opened book in the center of the
table and rests his left hand on the table and his right
hand on his knee as he leans forward. There is a long
pause.*)

MORIARTY. All that I have to say has already crossed
your mind. (*Pause.* HOLMES *takes the pipe out of his
mouth.*)

HOLMES. Then my answer has already crossed yours.
(*He puts his pipe back into his mouth. Pause.*)

MORIARTY. You stand fast?

HOLMES. Absolutely. (MORIARTY *puts his left hand
to his right hand inside coat pocket.* HOLMES *grabs
the gun and raises it toward* MORIARTY. HOLMES *leans
on the table with his right elbow with the gun in his
right hand. Pause.* MORIARTY *takes out a small black
memorandum book.* HOLMES *puts the gun down.*)

MORIARTY. You crossed my path on the fourth of
September. On the twenty-third you incommoded me;
by the middle of October I was seriously inconve-
nienced by you; at the end of October, I was absolutely hampered in my plans; and now at the close of
November I find myself placed in such a position
through your continual persecution that I am in positive danger of losing my liberty. The situation is be-

coming an impossible one. (HOLMES *takes his pipe out of his mouth and places it on the* D. S. L. *side of the table. He puts his left hand on his knee and his right elbow still rests on the table with his hand near the gun.*)

HOLMES. Have you any suggestion to make?

MORIARTY. You must drop it, Mr. Holmes, you really must.

HOLMES. After Monday.

MORIARTY. I am quite sure that a man of your intelligence will see that there can be but one outcome to this affair. It is necessary that you should withdraw. You have managed things in such a way that we have only one recourse left. It has been an intellectual treat to me to see the way you have grappled with this affair, and I say unaffectedly, it would be a grief to me to be forced to take any extreme measure. You smile, sir, but I assure you that it really would.

HOLMES. Danger is part of my trade.

MORIARTY. This is not danger. This is inevitable destruction. You stand in the way not merely of an individual but of a mighty organization, the full extent of which you, with all your cleverness, have been unable to realize. (MORIARTY *starts to put his memorandum book into his left hand pocket.* HOLMES *grabs the revolver with both hands and points it at* MORIARTY.)

HOLMES. Get your hands down. (MORIARTY *does not lower his hands.*)

MORIARTY. Why, I was merely about to . . .

HOLMES. Well, merely don't do it. If you want to replace that memorandum book so badly we'll have someone replace it for you. (HOLMES *reaches over the books to the* U. S. C. *side of the table and picks up the hand bell and rings it.*) I always like to save my guests unnecessary trouble. (*Pause.* MORIARTY *slowly turns and looks* S. R. *and then slowly back to* S. L.)

MORIARTY. Does it not occur to you, Mr. Holmes, he may possibly have been detained?

HOLMES. It does. But I also observe that *you are in very much the same predicament.* (HOLMES *rings the bell again while still holding the revolver in his right hand pointed at* MORIARTY. *The* S. L. *door opens and* BILLY *comes in without his jacket and closes the door behind him. He stands* U. S. *of the table between* HOLMES *and* MORIARTY.)

BILLY. I beg pardon, sir, someone tried to 'old me, sir! (HOLMES *leans back in his chair, crosses his legs and still holds the revolver on* MORIARTY.)

HOLMES. It is quite evident, however, that he failed to do so.

BILLY. Yes, sir, 'e's got my coat, sir, but 'e 'asn't got *me!*

HOLMES. Billy!

BILLY. (*He moves closer to* HOLMES.) Yes, sir?

HOLMES. The gentleman that I am pointing out to you with this revolver desires to replace the memorandum book that he took from his right hand inside coat pocket into his left hand inside coat pocket. As he is quite clearly not himself today and the exertion might prove injurious, suppose you attend to it.

BILLY. Yes, sir. (BILLY *crosses* C. L. *above the table and* MORIARTY *to* MORIARTY'S *right side.* MORIARTY *offers the memorandum book to* BILLY *as he opens the right side of his cape.* BILLY *takes the memorandum book from him and starts to put it into* MORIARTY'S *right hand pocket.*)

HOLMES. No. (BILLY *stops and* MORIARTY *opens the left side of his cape and* BILLY *puts the memorandum book into the pocket and quickly pulls out a revolver and jumps back and runs above* MORIARTY *to the* U. S. *side of the table.*)

BILLY. Look at this, sir.

HOLMES. Quite so. Put it on the table. (BILLY *starts*

to put the revolver down on the table U. S. R. *side when* MORIARTY *makes a grab for it.* BILLY *jumps back with the revolver and runs* S. L. *around* HOLMES *and stands* D. S. L. *of* HOLMES *and places it on the* D. S. L. *side of the table.*)

BILLY. Shall I see if he's got another one sir?

HOLMES. (*He turns around to* BILLY.) Why, Billy, you do disappoint me; the gentleman has taken the trouble to inform you that he hasn't.

BILLY. When, sir?

HOLMES. When he made a snatch for this one. (HOLMES *looks at* MORIARTY *still holding his own revolver on* MORIARTY *as he puts* MORIARTY'S *revolver in his lap.*) Professor, do you think of anything else you'd like? (MORIARTY *does not reply.*) Any little thing that you've got, that you want while Billy's here? No! (HOLMES *turns to* BILLY.) Ah, I'm sorry, that's all, Billy. (*Pause.*)

BILLY. Thank you, sir. (BILLY *exits* S. L. *closing the door behind him.* HOLMES *holds* MORIARTY'S *revolver in his left hand in his lap.*)

HOLMES. Rather a rash project of yours, Moriarty . . . even though you have made the street secure in every respect. (HOLMES *holds* MORIARTY'S *revolver up in his left hand and slips his own revolver into his right hand pocket.*) To think of using that thing . . . so early in the evening and in this part of town. (HOLMES *drops* MORIARTY'S *revolver onto the large opened book on the table as he stands and moves* D. L. *with one foot on the platform and the other on stage level.*) I am afraid that in the pleasure of this conversation I am neglecting business which awaits me elsewhere.

MORIARTY. Ah, well, well. (MORIARTY *stands up and picks up his hat off the table and holds it in front of him.*) It seems a pity, but I have done what I could. I know every move of your game. You hope to place me in the dock. I tell you that I will never stand in the dock. You hope to beat me. I tell you that you will never beat me. And if you are clever enough to bring destruction on me, rest assured I shall do as much to you.

HOLMES. (*He picks up his pipe from the* D. S. L. *side of the table.*) You have paid me several compliments, Moriarty, let me pay you one in return when I say that if I were assured of your destruction I would, in the interests of the public, cheerfully accept my own. (HOLMES *puts his pipe in his mouth. He checks his pockets for matches and finds none. He goes* U. C. *to the mantle to look for matches.* MORIARTY *drops his hat over the revolver that is on the books and then walks above the table to the* U. L. *side of the table.*)

MORIARTY. I came here this evening to see if *peace* could not be arranged between us.

HOLMES. (*He is still trying to find matches.*) Ah, yes. I saw that. That's rather good. (MORIARTY *picks up his hat and the revolver that's under it and holds both in front of him hiding the revolver.* HOLMES *picks up a box of matches and comes* D. C. *near the* U. R. *side of the table.*)

MORIARTY. You have seen fit not only to reject my proposals, but to make insulting references coupled with threats of arrest.

HOLMES. Quite so! Quite so! (HOLMES *lights a match and starts to light his pipe.*)

MORIARTY. Well, you do not heed my warning . . . (MORIARTY *uncovers his revolver and points it to the back of* HOLMES' *head.*) perhaps you will heed this! (MORIARTY *pulls the trigger. The revolver is empty.* HOLMES *turns and takes his left hand out of his dressing gown pocket and drops bullets into the bowl that is on the* S. R. *side of the table and then tosses his match away as he turns* S. R.)

HOLMES. Billy!

BILLY. (*He enters* S. L. HOLMES *has his back to the audience.*) Yes, sir!

HOLMES. Show this gentleman nicely to the door.

BILLY. Yes, sir! This way, sir! (BILLY *holds the door open for* MORIARTY. MORIARTY *drops the revolver onto the table and then puts his hat on his head. He stares at* HOLMES.)

MORIARTY. Touche, Mr. Holmes. Auf Weidersehen. (MORIARTY *turns and moves* S. L. *to the doorway where he grabs* BILLY *by the jaw . . . pause . . . then taps him gently on the cheek. Finally exits* S. L. BILLY *closes the door and turns back to* HOLMES. HOLMES *turns front and moves slowly* D. C. *holding his pipe.*)

HOLMES. Billy!

BILLY. (*He goes to the* U. S. R. *side of the table.*) Yes, sir!

HOLMES. Billy! You are a good boy.

BILLY. Yes, sir! Thank you, sir!

HOLMES. Now get me a cab to go to Waterloo Place. (HOLMES *puts his pipe into his mouth, takes out a box of matches, strikes a match and lights his pipe.* BILLY *salutes* HOLMES *with his left hand and the lights fade leaving a shadow of* HOLMES *above the* S. L. *door lighting his pipe and the CURTAIN comes down on famous silhouette.*)

BILLY. Yes, sir!

(*SOUND of a horse carriage is heard.*)

CURTAIN

ACT TWO

OPENING LINK SCENE

An Old Chinaman *enters from* d. l. *and moves* d. s. l.
The Karate Expert *enters* d. l. *and moves* c. s.
looking s. r. *and then* s. l. *The* Old Chinaman
beckons the Karate Expert *to him. The* Karate
Expert *goes to him and stands with his back
to the audience with his arms folded across his
chest.* Two Sailors *enter from* d. r. *and cross*
d. s. l. *to the* Old Chinaman *who gives them a
packet of dope. The* Two Sailors *move* d. c. *to
sample the packet as* Lightfoot McTague *is
heard singing from the* s. r. *pit as he enters onto
the stage.* McTague *sees the* Two Sailors *and
pushes himself between them and starts toward
the* Old Chinaman. *The* Karate Expert *stops*
McTague *with a karate leap. Pause.*

The Two Sailors *jump* McTague *knocking him to the
ground* d. r. c., *punching and kicking him. The*
Karate Expert *looks to the* Old Chinaman *who
signals him to follow. They exit* d. l. *into the fog.*
John *enters from* d. r. *and stops the fight. The*
Two Sailors *run off* d. l. McTague *stands up and
starts to laugh.* John *stands* s. l. *of him and
shoves him on the right shoulder which pushes*
McTague *off-balance and backwards* d. r. Mc-
Tague *starts to protest but* John *gives him another shove. BLACKOUT.*

They exit d. r. *In the BLACKOUT,* McTague *starts
to sing as he finds his way up the backstair way
to the entrance into the gas chamber. LIGHTS
UP.*

McTAGUE. (*Singing.*)
WE KISSED OUR WIVES WHEN WE
    RETURNED
WHO LONG FOR US DID WAIT
AND HE THAT'S SINGLE NEED NOT
    MOURN
HE WILL NOT NEED A MATE

YOUNG WOMEN STILL ARE WONDROUS
    KIND . . .

(McTAGUE *opens the door to the gas chamber and enters onto the balcony that leads to the circular staircase. He looks down at* LEARY *and* CRAIGIN.)

ACT TWO

SCENE 1

THE GAS CHAMBER AT STEPNEY

A large, dark, grimy room of an old building backing on wharves, etc. The only light in the room on the rise of the curtain is from a dim safety lamp. CRAIGIN *is sitting* S. L. *on a box holding a rope with which he is tying a hangman's knot.* LEARY *is sitting on the* D. S. R. *corner of the table looking at a magazine. The table is set* U. S. C. *under the window. A chair is on the* S. L. *side of the table with the safety lamp on the seat of the chair.* LEARY *turns the safety lamp on as the CURTAIN goes up. There is another chair at the* S. R. *side of the table upon which* LEARY *can rest one of his feet. The door opens at the top of the circular staircase and* McTAGUE *enters and moves down onto the first and second steps, leans over the rail looking at* CRAIGIN *and* LEARY.

McTAGUE. Here we are then.

LEARY. What's McTague doing 'ere?

McTAGUE. I was sent 'ere.

LEARY. I thought the Seraph was with us in this job.

CRAIGIN. 'E ain't. (McTAGUE *comes down the stairs and moves toward* LEARY *who moves* D. S. *toward him.* McTAGUE *pulls out his pocket knife and holds it ready for* LEARY. *Pause.* LEARY *hits* McTAGUE'S *right hand which has the knife in it and* McTAGUE *backs off* D. S. R.

LEARY. Who was the last person you put the gas on in this place?

CRAIGIN. I never 'eard 'is name. 'E'd been 'olding' back money on a job out some railway place.

McTAGUE. (*He folds the knife blade away and puts the knife in his right vest pocket.*) What's this 'ere job he wants done?

CRAIGIN. I ain't been told.

LEARY. As long as it's 'ere we know what it's likely to be. (LEARY *mimes turning a wheel to let the gas out.* McTAGUE *and* CRAIGIN *watch him and follow his gesture upward.* SIDNEY PRINCE *enters in the middle of this and they all stare at him. BEAT.* PRINCE *moves down onto the first and second steps of the circular staircase looking at the man.*)

PRINCE. Does any one of you blokes know if this is the place where I meet Alf Bassick? (McTAGUE *turns slowly* S. L. *to look at* CRAIGIN *as he sits on the second bottom step of the staircase. BEAT.*) From wot you say, I take it you don't.

CRAIGIN. We ain't knowin' no such man. 'E may be 'ere and 'e may not. (CRAIGIN *throws the rope he has been holding onto the floor* S. L.)

PRINCE. Oh! That's quite right then, thank you. (*BEAT.* PRINCE *comes down the stairs.* McTAGUE *is blocking his way and gets up after* PRINCE *stops behind him.* PRINCE *starts to move* C. S. *as* McTAGUE *and* LEARY *move in on him.* PRINCE *shoves his way past them.* MCTAGUE *moves* S. R. *and* LEARY *goes up to the table* S. R. *corner.*) Nice old place to find, this 'ere is. (PRINCE *takes out a cigarette case and takes a cigarette and puts it in his mouth then reaches into his pocket and takes out a box of matches.*) And when you do find it, I can't say it's any too cheerful. (PRINCE *takes a match and is about to strike it.*)

CRAIGIN. Here! (PRINCE *drops his match and all the matches in the match box onto the floor.*) Don't light that! It ain't safe! (*BEAT.* PRINCE *glances about.*)

PRINCE. If it ain't seekin' too much, wot's the matter with the place? It looks all roight to me.

CRAIGIN. Well, don't light no matches, and it'll stay lookin' the same. (*BEAT. The door opens and* BASSICK *enters.*)

BASSICK. Oh, there you are, Prince. I was looking for you outside. (BASSICK *comes down the staircase and moves* C. L. *toward* CRAIGIN *who is still sitting on the box* S. L. *on the edge of the platform unit.*)

PRINCE. You told me to be 'ere, sir. That was 'ow the last arrangement stood.

BASSICK. Very well! Have you got the rope, Craigin? (PRINCE *moves* D. S. R. *and stands behind the circular staircase next to the boiler unit.*)

CRAIGIN. It's 'ere.

BASSICK. That you, Leary?

LEARY. 'Ere, sir!

BASSICK. And McTAGUE?

MCTAGUE. 'Ere, sir!

BASSICK. You want to be very careful with it tonight. You've got a tough one.

CRAIGIN. You ain't said who, as I've 'eard.

BASSICK. Sherlock Holmes. (CRAIGIN *gets up and moves toward* BASSICK *as* LEARY *moves down to* BASSICK *and* MCTAGUE *moves behind* LEARY.)

CRAIGIN. You mean that, sir?

BASSICK. Indeed, I do!

CRAIGIN. We're goin' to count 'im out.

BASSICK. Well, if you *don't* and he gets away, I'm sorry for you, that's all.

CRAIGIN. I'll be a bit pleased to put the gas on 'im, I tell you *that*.

LEARY. Interfering stuck up nob, with . . . (LEARY *grabs hold of* BASSICK *by his lapels and pulls him up onto his toes.*)

BASSICK. Sh! Professor Moriarty's coming.

LEARY. Not the guv'nor? (BASSICK *pulls himself away from* LEARY *and moves* D. R. C. *off the platform.*)

BASSICK. Yes. He wanted to see to this. (*He looks up toward the door which opens and* MORIARTY *enters onto the balcony.* McTAGUE *moves* S. L. *to hide behind* CRAIGIN *who is standing in front of the boxes.* LEARY *moves up to the* D. S. L. *corner of the table. Pause.*)

MORIARTY. Where's Craigin?

CRAIGIN. 'Ere, sir. (MORIARTY *starts down the stairs.* JOHN *and* LARRABEE *enter onto the balcony platform.* LARRABEE *moves to the* S. R. *end and* JOHN *closes the door and stands at the* S. L. *end of the platform.*)

MORIARTY. Have you got your men? (MORIARTY *comes down the stairs and moves* C. S.)

CRAIGIN. All 'ere, sir.

MORIARTY. No *mistakes* tonight, Craigin.

CRAIGIN. That's right, sir.

MORIARTY. (*He glances about the chamber.*) Bassick, that door.

BASSICK. (*He runs* U. R. *to the cupboard door and opens and closes it to check it.*) A small cupboard, sir.

MORIARTY. No outlet? (BASSICK *moves* D. S. *to* MORIARTY.)

BASSICK. None whatever, sir.

MORIARTY. That window? (LEARY *goes* U. C. *to the window and swings the safety lantern in front of it so* MORIARTY *can check it.*)

BASSICK. Nailed down, sir!

MORIARTY. A man might break the glass.

BASSICK. If he did that he'd come against heavy iron bars outside.

CRAIGIN. We'll 'ave 'im tied down afore 'e could break any glass, sir.

MORIARTY. Ah! You've used it before. Of course, you know if it is air-tight?

BASSICK. Every crevice is caulked, sir.

MORIARTY. And the gas? (*All look up slowly.*) When the men turn the gas on him they leave by that door?

BASSICK. Yes, sir.

MORIARTY. It can be made quite secure?

BASSICK. Heavy bolts on the outside, sir, and solid bars over all.

MORIARTY. Let me see how quick you can operate them.

BASSICK. They tie the man down, sir. There's no need to hurry.

MORIARTY. Let me see how quick you can operate them.

BASSICK. Leary!

LEARY. Yes, sir! (LEARY *hands the safety lamp to* CRAIGIN *as he runs up the stairs, out the door, closes it and bolts it shut.* JOHN *bangs three times on the door to show that it is securely locked.*)

MORIARTY. Craigin, you will take your men outside that door and wait till Mr. Larrabee has had a little business interview with the gentleman. Take them up that passage to the left so that Holmes does not see them as he comes in. (CRAIGIN *moves* S. L. *giving the safety lamp to* McTAGUE. CRAIGIN *stands behind* Mc-TAGUE.) Who's driving the cab tonight? (LEARY *re-enters and closes the door then he comes down the staircase and stands* D. S. *of the cupboard door.*)

BASSICK. I sent O'Hagan. His orders are to drive him about for an hour, so he doesn't know the distance or the direction he's going, and then stop at the small door at Upper Swandem Lane. He's going to show him out there and show him up to this door.

MORIARTY. The cab windows are covered, of course?

BASSICK. Wooden shutters, sir, bolted and secure. There isn't a place he can see through the size of a pin. And there's the fog.

MORIARTY. Ah! We must have a lamp here. (CRAIGIN *moves* C. S. *to* MORIARTY *with the safety lamp.*)

BASSICK. Better not, sir. There might be some gas left.

MORIARTY. You've got a lamp there.

BASSICK. That's a safety lamp, sir. (MORIARTY *quickly puts his cane up onto* BASSICK'S D. S. *shoulder close to his neck.*)

MORIARTY. Oh, that's a safety lamp sir! The moment he sees that he will know what we're up to and we're finished. (MORIARTY *takes his cane off of* BASSICK'S *shoulder.*) There's no gas here. Go and tell the Lascar we must have a good lamp. (BASSICK *runs up the staircase and exits closing the door behind him.*) Bring that table over here. (MORIARTY *goes to the cupboard door and opens and closes it.* CRAIGIN *puts the safety lamp on the top box* S. L. LEARY *and* McTAGUE *get the table and move it* D. S. *and put it at a slight diagonal with the* D. S. L. *side* D. S. LEARY *puts the* S. R. *chair at the* S. R. *end of the table and* CRAIGIN *takes the* S. L. *chair that has been sitting on top of the table and puts it at the* S. L. *side of the table.* LEARY *stands above the* U. L. *corner of the table;* CRAIGIN *stands at the* U. R. *corner of the table and* McTAGUE *stands behind* CRAIGIN. MORIARTY *moves to* CRAIGIN *above the table.*) Now, Craigin, and the rest of you. One thing remember.No shooting tonight! Not a single shot. It can be heard in the alley below. (BASSICK *re-enters carrying an oil lamp.*) The first thing is to get his revolver away from him. Two of you attract his attention in front . . . (BASSICK *comes down the staircase.*)

The other come up on him from behind and snatch it out of his pocket. (CRAIGIN *nudges* McTAGUE. BASSICK *reaches the bottom of the stairs.*) Then you have him. Is that clear, Craigin?

CRAIGIN. I'll attend to it, sir. (LARRABEE *starts down the staircase and stands* D. S. R. *of the stairs.* BASSICK *moves to the table and puts the oil lamp center on the table.*)

BASSICK. Put out that lamp. (McTAGUE *grabs the safety lamp off the* S. L. *box.*)

CRAIGIN. Stop! (McTAGUE *gives the safety lamp to* CRAIGIN.) We'll want this when the other's taken away.

BASSICK. He mustn't see it, understand.

MORIARTY. Don't put it out. Cover it with something.

CRAIGIN. Here! Them boxes.

(McTAGUE *slides the boxes* U. L. *to* LEARY *who puts them* L. C. *of the window. The third box* McTAGUE *hands to* LEARY *who puts it on top of the other two boxes.* CRAIGIN *puts the safety lamp behind boxes.* [*1st* S. R. *Box—slides; 2nd Top—pick up; 3rd* S. L. *Box—pick up.*])

BASSICK. You mustn't stay any longer, Sir. O'Hagan might be a little early. That will do.

MORIARTY. (*He moves around the* U. R. *corner of the table and* D. R. *to* LARRABEE.) Mr. Larrabee, you understand! They are waiting for you.

LARRABEE. I understand, sir. (LEARY *stands at the* U. L. *corner of the table;* McTAGUE *is* D. S. *of him; and* CRAIGIN *is at the* D. R. *corner of the table.* BASSICK *goes up the stairs.*)

MORIARTY. I give you this opportunity to get what you can for your trouble. But anything that is found on him after you have finished . . . is subject to the usual division.

LARRABEE. That's all I want.

MORIARTY. When you have quite finished and got your money, suppose you blow that little whistle which I observe hanging from your watch chain and these gentlemen with take *their* turn. (MORIARTY *goes up the staircase and stops on the 2nd and 3rd steps from the top.*) And, Craigin . . .

CRAIGIN. Sir?

MORIARTY. At the proper moment present my compliments to Mr. Sherlock Holmes and say that I wish him a pleasant journey to the other side. (BASSICK *and* MORIARTY *exit.* LARRABEE *moves* U. C. *above the table.*)

LARRABEE. You'd better put that rope out of sight. (MCTAGUE *picks up the rope off the floor* S. L. *and moves* S. R. *onto the stairs.* CRAIGIN *crosses* S. R. *down stage of the table.* LEARY *goes* S. R. *and up the stairs and opens the door.*)

CRAIGIN. You understand, sir, we'll be just around the far turn of the passage so 'e won't see us as 'e's comin' up.

LARRABEE. I understand. (CRAIGIN *is half way up the stairs and stops.*)

CRAIGIN. An' it's w'en we 'ears that whistle, eh? (PRINCE *moves* U. S. *and stands behind the* S. R. *chair at the table.*)

LARRABEE. When you hear that whistle. (LEARY *exits first followed by* MCTAGUE *then* CRAIGIN. *The door closes.*)

PRINCE. Look 'ere, Jim, this sort of thing ain't so much in my line.

LARRABEE. I suppose not.

PRINCE. When it comes to blowing a safe or drillin' into bank vaults, I feel perfectly at 'ome, but I don't care so much to see a man . . . well, it ain't my line!

LARRABEE. (*He puts the package into his left hand pocket.*) Here! All I want you to do is go out to the corner of the street and let me know when he comes.

PRINCE. 'Ow will I let you know?

LARRABEE. Have you got a cab whistle?

PRINCE. Cert'nly.

LARRABEE. Well, when you see O'Hagan driving with him, come down the alley there and blow it twice.

PRINCE. Yes, but ain't it quite loikely to call a cab at the same time?

LARRABEE. What more do you want . . . take the cab and go home.

PRINCE. Oh, then you won't need me 'ere again?! (*He starts up the staircase.*)

LARRABEE. No.

PRINCE. (*He stops near the top of the stairs.*) Oh, very well then, I'll tear myself away.

(PRINCE *exits closing the door behind him.* LARRABEE *sits at the table,* S. L. *side, takes out his cigar case, take a cigar from it and lays the case, opened, on the table. He puts the cigar in his mouth as he takes out a box of matches. He takes a match and starts to strike it when he realizes what he's doing and stops. The door opens and* ALICE FAULKNER *enters.* LARRABEE *stands up as she moves down onto the first and second steps.*)

LARRABEE. How did you get to this place?

ALICE. I followed you in a cab.

LARRABEE. What have you been doing since I came up here? Informing the police, perhaps.

ALICE. I was afraid he'd come, so I waited.

LARRABEE. (*He slides the* S. L. *chair under the table.*) Oh, to warn him very likely?

ALICE. Yes, to warn him.

LARRABEE. (*He moves above the table moving toward the* U. S. R. *corner of the table.*) Then it's just as well you came up.

ALICE. I came to make sure . . .

LARRABEE. Of what?

ALICE. (*She comes down the stairs.*) You're going to

swindle and deceive him. I know that. *Is there anything more?*

LARRABEE. What could you do if there was?

ALICE. I could buy you off. Such men as you are always open to sale.

LARRABEE. How much would you give?

ALICE. The genuine package. The real ones. All the proofs . . . everything. (LARRABEE *moves to* ALICE s. R. *near the foot of the stairs.*)

LARRABEE. Have you got it with you?

ALICE. No, but I can get it.

LARRABEE. (*He moves around to the* D. S. C. *side of the table and sits on the edge of it.*) Oh, so you'll do all that for this man, would you? You think he's your friend, I suppose?

ALICE. I haven't thought of it.

LARRABEE. Look what he's doing now. Coming here to buy those things off me. (ALICE *steps onto the platform unit moving toward the table.*)

ALICE. They're false. They're counterfeit.

LARRABEE. He thinks they're genuine, doesn't he? He'd hardly come here to buy them if he didn't.

ALICE. He *may* ask my permission still.

LARRABEE. Ha! He won't get the chance.

ALICE. Won't get the chance. Then there *is* something else.

LARRABEE. Something else! Why, you see me here by myself, don't you?

ALICE. Where are those men who came up here?

LARRABEE. What men?

ALICE. Three villainous looking men. I saw them go in at the street door.

LARRABEE. Oh, those men. They went up the other stairway. You can see them in the next building, if you look out of that window. (LARRABEE *indicates the window* U. C. ALICE *goes* U. C. *to look out of the window. As she turns to go toward the staircase,* LARRABEE *moves* U. R. C. *between the* U. S. R. *corner of the table*

and the cupboard blocking ALICE *from the stairs.*
ALICE *stops in front of him.*)

ALICE. I'll look in the passageway, if you please.

LARRABEE. Yes, but I don't please.

ALICE. You wouldn't *dare* to keep me here. (LAR-
RABEE *reaches for his whistle that is attached to his
watch chain.*)

LARRABEE. I might *dare* but I won't. *You'd be in the
way.* (LARRABEE *takes his whistle and blows it several
times.*)

ALICE. Where are those men?

LARRABEE. Stay just where you are and you'll see
them very soon. (*The door opens and* CRAIGIN *and*
McTAGUE *enter and move down onto the staircase.*
LEARY *enters closing the door and stands on the* S. L.
edge of the balcony platform. ALICE *looks up at them.*)

ALICE. I knew it. (ALICE *turns* S. L. *and runs to the
boxes under the window* U. C. L. *and grabs hold of a
piece of pipe that is in the opened box. She turns* U. S.
*facing the window and raises the pipe in her right
hand as if to smash out the window panes.* LARRABEE
*moves to her grabbing hold of her right arm and swing-
ing her around to the* S. R. *side of him as he takes the
pipe away from her.* CRAIGIN *and* McTAGUE *run down
the staircase followed by* LEARY. McTAGUE *is holding
a rope that will be used to tie up* ALICE. McTAGUE
stands D. S. R. *of the staircase;* CRAIGIN *stands* U. S. *of
him with his back to the staircase;* LEARY *stands at the
bottom of the staircase.* ALICE *turns to look at them
and then turns to* LARRABEE.) Ah! You're going to do
him some harm! (LEARY *sits on the bottom two steps.*)

LARRABEE. Oh no, it's just a little joke at his expense.

ALICE. You wanted the letters, the package I had
in the safe! (LARRABEE *tosses the pipe back into the
box* U. C. L. ALICE *moves toward him and stands at the*
U. R. *corner of the table facing* LARRABEE.) I'll get it
for you. Let me go and I'll bring it here . . . I won't
say anything to anyone . . . not to him . . . not to
the policemen . . . not *anyone!*

LARRABEE. You needn't take the trouble to *get* it, but you *can tell me where it is* . . . and you better be quick about it too . . .

ALICE. Yes, if you'll promise not to go on with this.

LARRABEE. Of course! That's understood.

ALICE. You promise!

LARRABEE. Certainly I promise. Now where is it?

ALICE. Just outside my bedroom window . . . just outside on the left, fastened between the shutter and the wall. You can easily find it.

LARRABEE. Yes, I can easily find it.

ALICE. Now tell them . . . tell them to go.

LARRABEE. She mustn't get back to the house . . . not till I've been there. Tie her up and keep her outside. (LARRABEE *moves* D. S. L.)

CRAIGIN. Go an' get a hold, Leary. Hand me a piece of that rope. (MCTAGUE *hands him the rope and takes out a handkerchief from his pocket to use as a gag.* LEARY *gets up and starts to move toward* ALICE *above the table.*)

ALICE. (*She moves* D. L. *to* LARRABEE.) You said . . . you said if I *told* you . . .

LARRABEE. Well, we haven't done him any harm yet, have we? (ALICE *turns* S. R. *toward* CRAIGIN *and* MC-TAGUE. LEARY *stops above the table.*)

ALICE. Then send them away.

LARRABEE. Certainly. Go away now, boys, there's no more work for you tonight. (LEARY *starts to move toward* ALICE *as* CRAIGIN *and* MCTAGUE *move toward her crossing* D. S. *of the table.*)

ALICE. They don't obey you. They are . . . (*As she is about to scream,* LEARY *grabs her from behind and holds her as* MCTAGUE *puts the gag into her mouth while* CRAIGIN *ties her wrists with the rope.* [The rope used to tie her is a soft rope not the hemp rope Mc-Tague took off earlier.] *A WHISTLE is heard from* U. S. R. *It blows once . . . BEAT . . . then again.*)

CRAIGIN. Now out of the door with her.

LARRABEE. By God, he's *here.*
CRAIGIN. What?!
LARRABEE. That's Sid Prince. I put him on the watch.
CRAIGIN. We won't have time to get her out.
LARRABEE. Shut her up in that cupboard. (McTAGUE *crosses* D. S. *of the table to the cupboard door* U. R. *of the circular staircase.* LEARY *and* CRAIGIN *move* ALICE *toward the cupboard door.*)
LEARY. Yes, that'll do.
CRAIGIN. In with her. Open that door! Open that door!

(LEARY *goes to the door.* McTAGUE *crosses to door and tries to open it, then* LEARY *crosses to door and shoves* McTAGUE *out of the way and opens the door.* ALICE *hits* CRAIGIN *with her hand bag on the back of his head.* CRAIGIN *falls onto the table catching himself from falling to the floor.* ALICE *breaks away from him and runs* D. S. R. *and behind the circular staircase.* LEARY *runs after her followed by* CRAIGIN. McTAGUE *goes up onto the staircase and tries to grab her. She turns and pushes* LEARY *out of her way. He falls to the floor. She turns to run for the staircase and is confronted by* CRAIGIN. LEARY *gets up and stands behind her. She looks at* CRAIGIN *and faints into* LEARY'S *arms.* McTAGUE *opens the cupboard door and* LEARY *puts her inside the cupboard and closes the door.* McTAGUE *moves up onto the staircase.*)

LEARY. There ain't no lock on this 'ere door.
LARRABEE. No lock!
LEARY. No.
LARRABEE. Drive something in.
CRAIGIN. Here, this knife. (*He goes to* LEARY *handing him a large jackknife with the blade opened.*)

LARRABEE. A knife won't hold it. (MᴀTᴀGUE *runs up the stairs to keep a watch on the door.*)

CRAIGIN. Yes, it will. Drive it in strong.

LEARY. (*He forces the blade into the frame of the door.*) 'E'll have to find us 'ere.

CRAIGIN. Yes, and he won't, either. We'll go and do 'im up. (*He starts up the stairs.*)

LARRABEE. No, you won't. (CRAIGIN *stops on the stairs and looks at* LARRABEE.) I'll see him first, if you please.

MCTAGUE. Them was orders, Craigin.

LEARY. So it was.

MCTAGUE. There might be time to get back in the passage. He ain't gone up one flight yet

(MCTAGUE *exits first followed by* CRAIGIN *then* LEARY *who closes the door behind him.* LARRABEE *grabs a wooden block from the box* U. C. L. *and taps the knife in the door frame; then he throws the block back into the box and sits in the* S. L. *chair at the table; he picks up a cigar as* SHERLOCK HOLMES *enters and closes the door behind him then moves down onto the 2nd and 3rd steps.*)

HOLMES. How the devil is it that you crooks always manage to hit on the same places for your scoundrelly business? Well! I certainly thought, after all this driving about in a closed cab you'd show me something new.

LARRABEE. Seen it before, have you? (HOLMES *moves down onto the 4th and 5th steps then turns back to look at* LARRABEE.)

HOLMES. Well, I should think I have. I nabbed a friend of yours in this place while he was trying to drop himself out of that window. Ned Colvin, the Cracksman.

LARRABEE. Colvin. I never heard of him before.

HOLMES. No? Ha! Ha! Well, you certainly never

heard of him after. (HOLMES *comes down the rest of the stairs and moves to the* S. R. *side of the table with his hands in his pockets.*) A brace of counterfeiters used these regal chambers in the spring of '90. One of them hid in the cupboard.

LARRABEE. Times have changed since then.

HOLMES. (*He moves around above the table checking the cupboard door.*) So they have, Mr. Larrabee, so they have. Then it was only cracksmen, counterfeiters, and petty swindlers of various kinds. Now . . .

LARRABEE. Well? What now?

HOLMES. (*He stands behind the* U. S. R. *side of the table.*) Well, between you and me, Mr. Larrabee, we've heard some not altogether agreeable rumors; rumors of some pretty shady work not too far from here . . . and I've always had a suspicion . . . (HOLMES *moves* U. C. *to the window and runs his fingers over the frame and smells his finger tips as he moves* D. R. *of the table.*) my surmise was correct . . . it is.

LARRABEE. It is what?

HOLMES. Caulked.

LARRABEE. What does that signify to us?

HOLMES. Nothing to us, Mr. Larrabee, nothing to us, (HOLMES *pulls out the chair* S. R. *side of the table.*) but it might signify a good deal to some poor devil who's been caught in this trap.

LARRABEE. Well, if it's nothing to us, suppose we leave it alone and get to business. My time is limited.

HOLMES. Quite so, of course. (HOLMES *folds his arms in front of him.*) I should have realized that these reflections could not possibly appeal to you. But I take a deep interest in anything that pertains to what are known as the criminal classes and this same interest makes me particularly anxious to learn how you happened to select this rather gruesome place for an ordinary business transaction. (HOLMES *turns to* LARRABEE.)

LARRABEE. I selected this place, Mr. Holmes, because

I thought you might not feel quite so much at home, as you did in my own house last night. (HOLMES *reaches over and takes a cigar from* LARRABEE'S *cigar case on the* U. S. L. *side of the table; then he picks up a match from the floor.*)

HOLMES. Oh, ha! There you make a singular miscalculation, Mr. Larrabee. I feel perfectly at home, Mr. Larrabee! Perfectly!

(HOLMES *strikes the match on a match box. Once the match is lit,* HOLMES *turns to* LARRABEE, *who has been holding a cigar in his hand, and lights* LARRABEE'S *cigar; then* HOLMES *turns front and lights his own cigar. He puffs on the cigar several times as he lights his cigar which causes the flame to shoot up several inches.* [*It helps if two matches are stuck together in order to achieve the effect more fully.*] HOLMES *tosses the match* S. R. *and sits in the* S. R. *chair at the table.* LARRABEE *takes out the package from his right hand coat pocket and place it down on the* D. S. L. *corner of the table.*)

LARRABEE. Here is the little package which is the object of this meeting. I haven't opened it yet, but Miss Faulkner assures me everything is there.

HOLMES. Then there is no need of opening it, Mr. Larrabee.

LARRABEE. Oh, well, I want to see you satisfied. (HOLMES *puffs on his cigar with his right hand resting on the back of the chair and his left hand on the table.*)

HOLMES. That is precisely the condition in which you now behold me. Miss Faulkner is a truthful young lady. Her word is sufficient.

LARRABEE. Very well. Now what shall we say, Mr. Holmes? Of course, we want a pretty large price for this Miss Faulkner is giving up everything. She would not be satisfied unless the result justified it.

HOLMES. Suppose, Mr. Larrabee, that as Miss Faulkner knows nothing whatever about this affair, we omit her name from the discussion.

LARRABEE. Who told you she knows nothing. (HOLMES *uncrosses his legs and shifts his position more toward* LARRABEE.)

HOLMES. You did. Every look, tone, gesture—everything you have said and done since I have been in this room has informed me that she has never consented to this transaction. It is a little speculation of your own. (*He crosses his legs.*)

LARRABEE. I suppose you think you can read me like a book.

HOLMES. No, like a primer. (*He puffs on his cigar.*)

LARRABEE. Well, let that pass. How much will you give?

HOLMES. (*He turns slightly* S. R. *leaning back in his chair smoking his cigar with his left hand on the table.*) A thousand pounds.

LARRABEE. I couldn't take it.

HOLMES. What do you ask?

LARRABEE. Five thousand. (HOLMES *turns toward* LARRABEE *putting his right hand on the table and his left elbow on the back of his chair.*)

HOLMES. I couldn't give it. (*He puffs on his cigar.*)

LARRABEE. Very well, Mr. Holmes. (*He stands up holding the package then puts it in his left hand pocket.*) I'm afraid we've had all this trouble for nothing.

HOLMES. Oh, don't say that, Mr. Larrabee! To me the occasion has been doubly interesting. I have not only had the pleasure of meeting you again, but I have also availed myself of the opportunity of making some observations regarding this place which may not come amiss.

LARRABEE. Why, I've been offered four thousand for this little . . . (*He puts the package down on the* D. S. L. *corner of the table.*)

HOLMES. Why didn't you take it?

LARRABEE. Because I intend to get more.

HOLMES. That is too bad.

LARRABEE. If they offered four thousand they'll give five.

HOLMES. On the contrary. They won't give anything.

LARRABEE. Why not?

HOLMES. They've turned the case over to me.

LARRABEE. Will you give me three thousand? (*Laughing,* HOLMES *stands and moves around to the back of his chair.*)

HOLMES. Strange as it may appear, Mr. Larrabee, my time is quite as limited as yours. (*He leans on the back of his chair.*) I have brought with me the sum of one thousand pounds, that is all that I wish to pay. If it is your desire to sell at this figure kindly apprise me of the fact at once. (LARRABEE *picks up the package from the table and puts it into his left hand pocket.*) If not . . . (HOLMES *turns* S. R. *and starts for the stairs.*) permit me to wish you a very good evening. (*Pause.*)

LARRABEE. Go on! You can have it. It's too small a matter to haggle over. (*He throw the package center onto the table.* HOLMES *reseats himself at the table taking a bunch of banknotes from his left hand pocket and counts out ten of the notes and removes them from under the band that holds the notes together.* LAR-RABEE *waches* HOLMES *count the notes,* LARRABEE *stands center behind the table.*) Oh, I thought you said just a thousand.

HOLMES. I did. This is it.

LARRABEE. You brought a trifle more, I see. (HOLMES *takes his cigar from his mouth and puts it down on the* D. S. R. *edge of the table.*)

HOLMES. I did not say I had not brought any more. (*He puts his left elbow down on the remaining notes on the table as he counts the ten in his hand.*)

LARRABEE. You can do your little tricks when it comes to it, can't you?

HOLMES. It depends on who I'm dealing with. (*He hands* LARRABEE *the ten one hundred pound notes and picks up the package from the table. He takes his elbow off the remaining notes on the table as he turns* S. R. *to examine the package.* LARRABEE *moves closer to the notes on the table and snatches them up. He laughs as he turns* S. L. *counting the notes.* HOLMES *tops* LARRABEE'S *laugh as he turns to watch* LARRABEE *with the notes.*) Now I've got you where I want you, Jim Larrabee! You've been very cunning, very cautious, very wise. We couldn't find a thing to hold you for; but this little slip will get you ten years for *robbery*.

LARRABEE. Oh! You'll have me in, will you? What are your views about being able to get away from here yourself?

HOLMES. I do not anticipate any particular difficulty.

LARRABEE. Perhaps you'll change your mind about that.

HOLMES. (*He stands and turns* S. R. *looking at the cupboard door. He moves around to the* U. S. R. *side of the table.*) Whether I change my mind or not, I certainly shall leave this place and your arrest will swiftly follow.

LARRABEE. My arrest? Ha, ha! Robbery, eh? Why, even if you got away from here you haven't got a witness. Not a witness to your *name*.

HOLMES. I'm not so sure of that, Mr. Larrabee! *Do you usually fasten* that door with a *knife?* (HOLMES *goes to the door and pulls out the knife throwing it to the floor as he throws open the door and sees* ALICE.)

LARRABEE. Come away from that door.

HOLMES. Stand back! (HOLMES *turns round to face* LARRABEE *stretching his arms across the doorway.*) You contemptible scoundrel! What does this mean?! (HOLMES *turns back to* ALICE *and picks her up into his arms and carries her to the* D. S. R. *chair next to the table. He puts her into the chair and kneels in front of her as he takes the gag out of her mouth and throws it onto the table. He unties her wrists and ankles and throws the rope onto the table. He rubs both her wrists and ankles where the rope has been tied.*)

LARRABEE. I'll show you what it means cursed quick. (LARRABEE *takes hold of his silver whistle and blows it several times.*)

HOLMES. I'm afraid you're badly hurt, Miss Faulkner.

(CRAIGIN *and* McTAGUE *open the door and enter moving down onto the first three steps observing* HOLMES. LEARY *follows them trying to crouch in the shadows and closing the door behind him.* ALICE *looks up at them.*)

ALICE. No! Mr. Holmes!!

HOLMES. (*He does not look around at them.*) Ah, Craigin, delighted to see you. And you too, McTague. I infer from your presence here at this particular juncture that I am not dealing with Mr. Larrabee *alone.*

LARRABEE. Your inference is quite correct, Mr. Holmes.

HOLMES. It is not difficult to imagine who is at the bottom of such a conspiracy as this. (HOLMES *stands up and helps* ALICE *up out of the chair. Both move* D. S. C. CRAIGIN *and* MCTAGUE *come down the stairs and move* D. S. *of the staircase.* LEARY *comes into view on the landing at the top of the stairs.* LARRABEE *holds his position at the* U. S. L. *corner of the table.*) I hope you're beginning to feel a little more yourself, Miss Faulkner, because we shall leave here very soon.

ALICE. Oh yes, do let us go, Mr. Holmes.

CRAIGIN. You'll 'ave to wait a bit. Mr. 'Omes. (CRAIGIN *moves toward* HOLMES *but keeps his distance.*

LEARY *starts to come down the stairs.*) There's a little matter of business we'd like to talk over. (LEARY *moves* s. l. *above the table.*)

HOLMES. Very well, Craigin, I'll see you tomorrow morning in your cell at Bow Street.

CRAIGIN. Werry sorry, sir, but I cawn't wait till morning. It's got to be settled tonight.

HOLMES. All right, Craigin, we'll settle it tonight. (HOLMES *turns* s. r. *to face* CRAIGIN. HOLMES *slips his right hand into right-hand coat pocket to prepare for taking out his revolver, which he will toss at the end of* CRAIGIN'S *next line.*) It's so werry himportant, Mr. 'Omes, so werry himportant indeed *that you'll 'ave to 'tend to it now.* (LEARY *grabs hold of* ALICE *and shoves her* u. s. *She ends up standing center* u. s. *of the table.* LARRABEE *moves toward the cupboard door.* SHERLOCK HOLMES *tosses his revolver over his* u. s. l. *shoulder;* LEARY *catches it and drops to his knees holding the revolver on* HOLMES.)

CRAIGIN. 'Ave you got his revolver?

LEARY. 'Ere it is.

HOLMES. (*He turns to* LEARY.) Ah, Leary! It needed only your blithe personality to make the party complete. (HOLMES *looks at* LARRABEE *and then* CRAIGIN *and* McTAGUE.) There is only one other I could wish to welcome here, and that is the talented author of this midnight carnival. We shall have him, however, by tomorrow night. (HOLMES *turns* u. s. r. *and moves to the chair* s. r. *of the table and sits and picks up the cigar from the edge of the table. He puts the cigar in his mouth and takes out his note pad and pencil and jots down several notes.* LEARY *moves* u. s. l. *still holding the revolver on* HOLMES. LEARY *kneels on one knee.* LEARY *is on a line level with* HOLMES. CRAIGIN *moves* u. s. r. *near the circular staircase.* McTAGUE *stays close to* CRAIGIN. ALICE *moves* s. r. *nearer to the cupboard door as* LARRABEE *counters to the* u. s. l. *corner of the table.*)

CRAIGIN. Though 'e ain't 'ere, Mr. 'Olmes, 'e gave me a message for yer. 'E presented his koindest compliments and wished yer a pleasant journey to the other side.

HOLMES. (*He continues to write with his cigar in his mouth.*) That's very kind of him, I'm sure.

LARRABEE. Writing your will, are you? (LARRABEE *moves* U. C. *in front of the window.* HOLMES *looks* D. S. R. *at* CRAIGIN *and* McTAGUE *and jots down some notes.*)

HOLMES. No. (*He takes the cigar out of his mouth and takes a quick glance at* LARRABEE . . . *looking him down and up . . . and jotting down the last of his notes.*) Just a brief description of one or two of you gentlemen for the police. They know the others. (*He puts the cigar back into his mouth and puts his note pad and pencil away.*)

LEARY. And when will you give it 'em, Mr. 'Omes?

HOLMES. In nine or nine and a half minutes. Mr. Leary.

LARRABEE. Leaving here in nine minutes, are you?

HOLMES. No. In one. It will take me eight minutes to find a policeman. This is a very dangerous neighborhood. (*He takes a puff on his cigar.*)

LARRABEE. Well, when you're ready to start, let us know.

HOLMES. (*He sits back in his chair.*) I'm ready now. (CRAIGIN, McTAGUE *and* LEARY *brace themselves for action.*)

CRAIGIN. I've an idea you won't be going anywhere, Mr. 'Omes, cause we're gonna tie yer down nice and tight to the top o' that table.

HOLMES. (*He stands and moves quickly* D. C.) Well, by Jove! I don't think you *will*. (HOLMES *turns and faces* U. S.) That's my idea, you know.

CRAIGIN. An' you'll save yourself a deal of trouble if ye submit quiet and easy like . . . because if ye don't ye moight get knocked about a bit . . . (ALICE

runs around the U. S. L. *side of the table and down to*
HOLMES. LEARY *counters to the* U. S. L. *side of the table*
still holding the revolver on HOLMES.)

ALICE. Oh, Mr. Holmes!

LARRABEE. Stay away from him! Come over here if
you don't want to get hurt.

HOLMES. My child, if you don't want to get hurt,
stay close to me. (*The two of them are facing* U. S.)

LARRABEE. Aren't you coming?

ALICE. No!

CRAIGIN. You'd better look out, Miss . . . he might
get killed.

ALICE. Then you can kill me too. (*There's a pause.*
HOLMES *takes a quick look at* ALICE. CRAIGIN *jumps*
in place as a signal for everyone to move. HOLMES *and*
ALICE *move* U. L. C. *near the large pipe.* ALICE *stays*
behind HOLMES. LEARY *moves to the* S. R. *side of the*
table and LARRABEE *moves up near the cupboard door.*
HOLMES *does not take his eyes off the men as He*
speaks to ALICE.)

HOLMES. I'm afraid you don't mean that, Miss
Faulkner.

ALICE. Yes, I *do.*

HOLMES. No. You would not say it at another time
or place.

ALICE. I would say it anywhere . . . always.

CRAIGIN. So you'll 'ave it out with us, eh?

HOLMES. Did you imagine for one moment, Craigin,
that I won't have it out with you? (CRAIGIN *gives the*
rope to McTAGUE *and moves more* C. S. *toward*
HOLMES.)

CRAIGIN. Well, then, I'll 'ave to give you one . . .
same as I did yer right 'and man this afternoon. (Mc-
TAGUE *stays close to* CRAIGIN. HOLMES *speaks to* ALICE
without turning to her or taking his eyes off from
CRAIGIN *and* McTAGUE.)

HOLMES. Ah! You heard him say that. *Same as he*
did my right-hand man this afternoon.

ALICE. Yes! Yes!

HOLMES. However unpleasant the experience, I ask you to remember that face. (HOLMES *points to* CRAIGIN. CRAIGIN *steps back turning* S. R. *trying to shield his face with his left hand.*) In three days time I shall ask you to identify it in the prisoner's dock. Yes, and the rest of you with him. You surprise me, gentlemen, thinking you are sure of anybody in this room and never once taking the trouble to look at that window. If you wanted to make it perfectly safe, you should have had those *missing bars put back.*

LARRABEE. Bars or no bars, you're not going to get out of here as easy as you expect.

HOLMES. (*He moves closer to the* S. L. *side of the table.*) There are so many ways, Mr. Larrabee, I hardly know which one to choose.

CRAIGIN. Well, you'd better choose quick . . . I can tell you that.

HOLMES. I'll choose at once . . . Mr. Craigin . . . (HOLMES *looks around the room.*) and my choice . . . (HOLMES *picks up the* S. L. *chair.*) falls on this. (HOLMES *smashes the chair down onto the table knocking the lamp onto the floor. BLACKOUT. The glow of* HOLMES' *cigar is all that should be visible.* ALICE *runs* S. R. *and up the staircase stopping at the top at the door.* HOLMES *moves the cigar about the room and sticks it in a hole* S. R. *of the window and then runs up the staircase and stops near the top.* CRAIGIN, MCTAGUE *and* LEARY *make a lot of noise with their feet as they cross* S. L. *below the table.*)

CRAIGIN. The cigar. Trace 'im by the cigar. (CRAIGIN, MCTAGUE *and* LEARY *cross* S. L.) Follow the cigar.

LARRABEE. Look out. He's going for the window. Get that light.

CRAIGIN. The safety lamp. Where is it? (*The lights come up.* CRAIGIN *picks up the safety lamp from behind the boxes* U. S. L. LEARY *has* MCTAGUE *by his hair with* MCTAGUE'S *head on the* U. S. L. *end of the table.* LEARY *stands to the right of* McTAGUE *with his arm raised to come down on* McTAGUE'S *head.* HOLMES *looks at all of them.*)

HOLMES. You'll find that cigar in a crevice by the window.

(ALICE *and* HOLMES *exit bolting the door behind them.* LEARY, CRAIGIN *and* McTAGUE *runs* S. R. *and up the staircase.* LEARY *bangs on the door.*)

BLACKOUT

ACT TWO

HURDY GURDY LINK GOING FROM SCENE ONE TO SCENE TWO

An ORGAN GRINDER *enters from* D. S. R. *singing "When Irish Eyes Are Smilin." When he reaches* C. S., *he stops and begins turning the handle on the organ. From* D. S. L., *a* NANNY *enters pushing a pram followed by* TWO HANDSOME GUARDSMEN. *She stops* D. L. C. *of the* ORGAN GRINDER, *leans over the pram to check the baby. The* GUARDSMEN *come and stand on either side of her.*)

NANNY. (*Nurse.*) Kootchy-kootchy-kootchy-koo!
GUARDSMEN. Kootchy-kootchy-kootchy-koo! (*The* NANNY *pushes the pram* D. S. *and around to the* D. S. R. *side stooping briefly to check the baby again. The* GUARDSMEN *look after her.*) Kootchy-kootchy-kootchy-koo!

(*The* S. R. GUARDSMAN *starts to follow her, stops briefly to listen* S. R. *of the* ORGAN GRINDER, *then exits* D. S. R. *The* S. L. GUARDSMAN *goes to the* S. L. *side of the* ORGAN GRINDER *and starts turning the handle of the organ.* BASSICK *enters from* D. S. R.

still dressed as an Inspector and followed by the
TRUMPETER *who stays* D. S. R. BASSICK *goes to
the* S. R. *side of the* ORGAN GRINDER.)

BASSICK. Come on now, move along there. (*The*
GUARDSMAN *stops turning the handle and stands at
attention.*) Try Buckingham Palace, soldier.

(*The* GUARDSMAN *does an about face and exits* D. S. R.
The ORGAN GRINDER *mutters something and exits*
D. S. R. BASSICK *turns to the* TRUMPETER *and
signals him to play.* BASSICK *exits* D. S. L. *while
the* TRUMPETER *plays and exits* D. S. L.)

ACT TWO

SCENE 2

In hall of Watson's house.

MRS. SMEEDLEY. Thank you very much for seeing
me, doctor, it's very kind indeed.
WATSON. What ever you do, don't make any mistake
about the medicine.
MRS. SMEEDLEY. Oh, no I won't. Would you hold
that, please. Green for 'er cough and brown for the
fever. (*She gives* DOCTOR WATSON *two coins and then
takes the medicine bottles back from* PARSONS.) Thank
you very much.
WATSON. If she's no better tomorrow you will let
me know, of course.
MRS. SMEEDLEY. Oh yes, doctor, I'll come myself.
WATSON. And whatever you do, don't let her out.
MRS. SMEEDLEY. Oh no, the fog would kill her.
WATSON. Good night, Mrs. Smeedley.
MRS. SMEEDLEY. Goodnight, doctor, thank you very
much. Goodnight, doctor. (*She exits* D. S. L. *As she
goes out we realise it is* MADGE *in disguise "casing the
joint."*)

WATSON. Parsons! That woman who just left, do you know her?

PARSONS. I can't say as I recollect 'avin' seen 'er before. Was there anything . . . ?

WATSON. Oh no! Acted a little strange, that's all. I thought I saw her looking about the hall before she went out.

PARSONS. Yes, sir, she did give a look. I saw that myself, sir.

WATSON. Oh, well, I dare say it was nothing. Is there anyone waiting, Parsons?

PARSONS. There's one person in the waiting-room, sir. A gentleman.

WATSON. I'll see him, but I've only a short time left. I have an important appointment at nine.

PARSONS. Very well, sir. Then you'll see this gentleman, sir?

WATSON. Yes. (DOCTOR WATSON *comes down off the steps as the SET REVOLVES to* DOCTOR WATSON'S *office.* WATSON *enters onto the set and sits at his desk* D. S. R. SIDNEY PRINCE *enters the office and* PARSONS *exits closing the double doors as he leaves.* PRINCE *speaks in a husky whisper.*)

PRINCE. Good evenin', doctor!

WATSON. Good evening. Pray be seated.

PRINCE. Thanks, I don't mind if I do. (*He sits in the chair that is* S. L. *of the desk. BEAT.* PRINCE *looks at* WATSON.)

WATSON. What seems to be the trouble.

PRINCE. Throat, sir. Most dreadful sore throat. The fog.

WATSON. Sore throat, eh?

PRINCE. It's the most 'arrowing thing I ever 'ad! It pains me that much to swallow that I . . .

WATSON. (*He stands and moves around the* U. S. *end of the desk and stands* S. L. *of* PRINCE.)

WATSON. Hurts you to swallow, does it?

PRINCE. Indeed it does. Why, I can 'ardly force a bit of food down 'cept for little tiddly morsels, an' a spot of calf's foot jelly. (WATSON *crosses* S. L. C. *to the examining chair.* PRINCE *stands and follows him.* WATSON *motions for* PRINCE *to get into the chair.* PRINCE *lies back in the chair.*)

WATSON. Just relax a moment. (PRINCE *goes back in the chair.*) Now, mouth open . . . wide as possible. (WATSON *takes a silver tongue depresser and examines* PRINCE'S *throat.*)

PRINCE. Eh!

WATSON. Say "ah!"

PRINCE. Ah!

WATSON. Where do you feel this pain?

PRINCE. Just about there, doctor, 'orrible. Inside about there.

WATSON. That's odd. I don't find anything wrong.

PRINCE. You may not foind anything wrong, but I feel it wrong. If you would only give me something to take away this awful agony. Pain, pain, nothin' but pain.

WATSON. Curious it should have affected your voice in this way. Well, I'll give you a gargle. It may help you a little.

PRINCE. Yes, if you only would, doctor.

(WATSON *goes into the dispensary* D. L. PRINCE *jumps out of the examining chair and runs to the windows* S. R. *He pulls up two of the window shades and waves his hat up and down as a signal then runs up to the double doors, opens one and looks out.* WATSON *comes out of the dispensary holding a brown medicine bottle and sees* PRINCE *at the door.*)

WATSON. What are you doing there?

PRINCE. Why, nothing at all, doctor. I felt such a

draught on the back o' my neck don't yer know, that I opened the door to see where it came from! (WATSON *croses* S. R. *to the* D. S. *side of his desk and taps the bell for* PARSONS *as he puts the medicine bottle on the* U. S. *end of the desk as he moves to the* S. R. *side of the desk.*)

WATSON. Parsons. (PARSONS *enters.*) Show this man the shortest way to the street and close the door after him.

PRINCE. But, doctor, ye don't understand.

WATSON. I understand quite enough. Good evening. (*He sits behind his desk.*)

PRINCE. Yer know, the draught plays hell with my throat, sir . . . I get this terrible shooting experience.

PARSONS. (*He moves behind* PRINCE *and starts to take hold of him.*) This way, sir, if you please. (PARSONS *takes* PRINCE *by the collar and the seat of his pants and starts to escort him out.*)

PRINCE. I consider that you've treated me damned outrageous, that's wot I do, and ye won't hear the last of this very soon. (PARSONS *exits* U. S. R. *with* PRINCE. PARSONS *returns after the DOOR SLAMS. He is carrying* WATSON'S *coat, hat and gloves. He stands* U. C.)

WATSON. I shall be at Mr. Holmes' in Baker Street. If there's anything special, you'll know where to send for me. (*He stands and looks at his pocket watch.*) The appointment was for nine. It's fifteen minutes past eight now. (WATSON *moves around the* U. S. *end of the desk and goes to* PARSONS *who holds his coat ready for him to get into it.*) I'm going to walk over. (*The front DOOR BELL RINGS.*) No, I won't see anybody else tonight. (WATSON *has his coat on and is holding his gloves and hat.*)

PARSONS. Yes, sir. (*He starts to exit* U. S. C. WATSON *looks* S. R. *and notices the two shades are up.*)

WATSON. Parsons! Why aren't those blinds down?

PARSONS. They was down only a few moments ago, sir!

WATSON. That's strange! Well, you'd better pull them down now.

PARSONS. Yes, sir. (PARSONS *goes* s. r. *to the windows. As he starts to pull down the first shade, the front DOOR BELL RINGS. As he pulls down the second shade, the DOOR BELL RINGS again.*)

WATSON. You'd better go see who it is! (PARSONS *exits* u. c. *and off* u. r. WATSON *goes to his desk and picks up the medicine bottle. The DOOR BELL STOPS RINGING.*)

PARSONS. Yes, sir. (WATSON *crosses* s. l. *and goes into the dispensary to put the medicine bottle away.* PARSONS *re-enters* u. c. *as* WATSON *comes out of the dispensary and starts to move* c. s.) If you please, sir, it isn't a patient at all, sir.

WATSON. Well, what is it?

PARSONS. A lady, sir . . . and she wants to see you most particular, sir!

WATSON. What does she want to see me about?

PARSONS. She didn't say, sir. Only she said it was of the utmost himportance to 'er, if you could see 'er, sir.

WATSON. Is she there in the hall?

PARSONS. Yes, sir.

WATSON. Very well, I was going to walk for the exercise but I can take a cab. (WATSON *takes off his coat and* PARSONS *takes it along with his hat and gloves.*)

PARSONS. Then you will see the lady, sir.

WATSON. Yes. And call a cab for me at the same time. Have it wait.

PARSONS. Yes, sir. (PARSONS *exits* u. c. *and off* u. r. WATSON *goes behind his desk* s. r. *and starts to sit just as* PARSONS *shows* MADGE LARRABEE *in.* PARSONS *exits closing the doors.* MADGE *is disguised as a society lady. She moves* d. s. c.)

MADGE. Ah! Doctor, it's awfully good of you to see me. I know what a busy man you must be. (PARSONS *closes the doors.*) But, I'm in *such* trouble. Oh, it's really too dreadful. You will excuse my troubling you in this way, won't you?

WATSON. (*He moves around to the* U. S. L. *end of his desk.*) Don't speak of it, madam.

MADGE. Oh, thank you so much! For it did look frightful my coming in like this, but I'm not alone, oh, no! I left my maid in the cab. I'm Mrs. M. de Witte Seaton. (*She attempts to find her card case in her hand bag.*) Dear me, I didn't bring my card case, or if I did I lost it.

WATSON. (*He goes to her and shows her a chair* D. L. *to sit in.*) Don't trouble about a card, Mrs. Seaton. (*She sits.* WATSON *goes* R. C. *and takes the chair that is* S. R. *of his desk and moves it* S. L. *near to* MADGE *and sits facing her.*)

MADGE. Oh, thank you. You don't know what I've been through this evening trying to find someone who could tell me what to do. It's something that's happened, doctor, it has just simply happened, I know that it wasn't his fault! I know it.

WATSON. Whose fault?

MADGE. My brother's . . . my poor, dear, youngest brother. He couldn't possibly have done such a thing, he simply couldn't, and . . .

WATSON. Such a thing as what, Mrs. Seaton?

MADGE. As to take the plans of our defences at Gibraltar from the Admiralty Offices. They think he stole them, doctor, and they've arrested him for it . . . you see, he works there. He was the only one who knew anything about them in the whole office because they trusted him so. He was to make copies and . . . oh, Doctor, it's really too dreadful!

WATSON. I'm terribly sorry, Mrs. Seaton . . .

MADGE. Oh, thank you so much! They told me you were Mr. Holmes' friend . . . several people told me that, several . . . they advised me to ask you where

I could find him . . . and everything depends on it, doctor . . . everything.

WATSON. Holmes, of course. He's just the one you want.

MADGE. That's *it!* He's just the one . . . and there's hardly any time left! They'll take my poor brother away to prison tomorrow!

WATSON. (*He stands up.*) There, there, Mrs. Seaton. Pray control yourself.

MADGE. Now what would you advise me to do?

WATSON. I would go to Holmes at once.

MADGE. But I've been. I've been and he wasn't *there!*

WATSON. You went to his house?

MADGE. Yes, in Baker Street. That's why I came to you! They said he might be here!

WATSON. No, he isn't here! (*He turns* S. R.)

MADGE. But don't you expect him some time this evening? (WATSON *turns back to* MADGE.)

WATSON. No. There's no possibility of his coming . . . so far as I know.

MADGE. But couldn't you *get* him to come? It would be such a great favor to me. I'm almost worn out with going about and with this dreadful anxiety! If you could get word to him to . . . to come.

WATSON. I could *not* get him to come, madam. And I beg you to excuse me. I am going out myself on urgent business. (WATSON *moves his chair back to the* U. S. L. *side of his desk* S. R. *as* MADGE *stands.*)

MADGE. Oh, certainly! Don't let me detain you! And you think I had better call at his house again?

WATSON. (*He rings the bell on his desk for* PARSONS.) That will be the wisest thing to do.

MADGE. Oh, thank you so much. You don't *know* how you've encouraged me! Well, good night, doctor. (MADGE *starts to go* U. C. *to exit through the double doors when the sound of a CAB CRASH is HEARD*

u. s. r. PARSONS *enters opening the double doors.* WATSON *moves behind his desk and stands.*)

WATSON. What's that, Parsons?

PARSONS. I really can't say, sir, but it sounded to me like a haccident. (MADGE *turns and moves* D. C.)

MADGE. Oh dear! I do hope it isn't anything serious!

WATSON. Probably nothing more serious than a broken-down cab. See what it is, Parsons.

PARSONS. There's the bell, sir! There's somebody 'urt, sir, an' they're a-wantin' *you!* (MADGE *crosses* S. R. *toward* WATSON *and stands between the* U. S. *end of the desk and the 3-fold screen* U. L.)

WATSON. Well, don't allow anybody to come in! (WATSON *moves* U. C. *toward the double doors.*) I have no more time.

PARSONS. Very well, sir. (PARSONS *exits leaving the double doors open. The BELL RINGING and DOOR BANGING stops. Several voices are heard shouting off stage* U. R. MADGE *moves closer to the windows as she watches* WATSON *at the doors.*)

* * * * *

(*Over-lap.*)

OFF STAGE VOICES. We 'ad to bring 'im in, man. There's nowhere else to go!

PARSONS. (*Off Stage* U. R.) The doctor can't see anybody.

OFF STAGE VOICES. Well, let the old gent lay 'ere awhile, can't yer. It's common decency. Wot 'ave yer got a red lamp 'angin' outside yer bloomin' door for? Yes! Yes, let him stay.

MADGE. But they're coming in, doctor.

WATSON. (*Going* U. C. *by double doors.*) Parsons! Parsons!

* * * * *

PARSONS. (*He enters while the off stage voices continue to ad lib.*) They would bring 'im in, sir. It's an old gentleman as was 'urt a bit w'en the cab upset!

WATSON. Let them put him here. Have that cab wait for me.

PARSONS. Yes, sir! (WATSON *moves to the operating chair* U. L. *as* PARSONS *exits* U. R. *to help the* OLD GENTLEMAN *into the office. The off stage voice fade away as we hear the* OLD GENTLEMAN *whining out complaints, threats and groans.* MADGE *moves to the* U. S. L. *end of the desk.*)

MADGE. Oh doctor, isn't it frightful.

WATSON. Mrs. Seaton, if you will be so good as to step this way.

MADGE. But I . . . I may be of some use, doctor.

WATSON. None whatever.

MADGE. But, doctor, I *must see the* poor fellow. I haven't the *power* to go!

WATSON. Madam, I believe you have some ulterior motive in coming here! You will kindly . . . (MADGE *moves* S. R. *and stands* U. S. R. *behind the 3-fold screen.* WATSON *starts toward her but* PARSONS *and* FORMAN *enter helping the* OLD GENTLEMAN *into the room.* WATSON *moves* S. L. *behind the examining chair.* PARSONS, *the* OLD GENTLEMAN *and* FORMAN *move* D. C. L. PARSONS *tries to hold the* OLD GENTLEMAN *back from going to the* D. L. *chair.* WATSON *moves to the* S. R. *side of the double doors. The* OLD GENTLEMAN *resists the help of* PARSONS *and* FORMAN.)

HOLMES. Oh, oh!

PARSONS. This way, sir! Be careful of the step, sir! Mind your leg, sir. Up we go. That's it.

DRIVER. Now we'll go in 'ere. You'll see the doctor an' it'll be all right.

HOLMES. No, it won't be all right. (HOLMES *tries to move to the* D. S. L. *chair but* PARSONS *keeps hold of him and tries to move* HOLMES *into the* U. L. *examining chair.*)

PARSONS. Now over to this chair.

HOLMES. No, I'll sit here.

PARSONS. No, this is the chair, sir.

HOLMES. Don't I know where I want to sit!

DRIVER. You'll sit 'ere. (*The* DRIVER *pushes* HOLMES *into the examining chair* U. L.) Now, the doctor'll have a look at ye. 'Ere's the Doctor.

HOLMES. That's not a doctor.

DRIVER. It is a doctor. (*The* DRIVER *turns to* WATSON, *who is* S. R. C.) 'Ere, doctor, will you just come and have a look at this old gent?

HOLMES. (*He grabs hold of* FORMAN.) Wait, wait, wait! Are you the driver?

DRIVER. Yes, I'm the driver.

HOLMES. Well, I'll have you arrested for this. (*He attempts to get up out of the examining chair but the* DRIVER *pushes* HOLMES *back into the chair.*)

DRIVER. You cawn't arrest me.

HOLMES. I can't, but somebody else can. You are a very disagreeable man! (HOLMES *turns to* PARSONS.) Are you a driver?

PARSONS. No, sir!

HOLMES. Well, what are you?

PARSONS. I'm the butler, sir.

HOLMES. *Butler! Butler!* A likely story.

* * * * *

(*Over-lap.*)

DRIVER. He's the doctor's servant.

WATSON. Parsons, go and see that that cab is waiting for me. (PARSONS *exits* U. C. *closing the doors and going off* U. R.)

HOLMES. Who asked you who he was?

DRIVER. Never mind who asked me. (HOLMES *attempts to get up out of the chair again but the* DRIVER *pushes him back into it.*) Sit down here! Sit down and be quiet.

*   *   *   *   *

HOLMES. Quiet! Quiet! Where's my hat? My hat! My hat!

DRIVER. There's your 'at in your 'and.

HOLMES. That isn't my hat! (*The DRIVER takes the hat and starts to exit u. c. when HOLMES grabs onto the back of his coat.*) Here, come back.

DRIVER. I cawn't stay around 'ere, you know! Some one'll be pinching my cab. (*The DRIVER exits u. c. and off u. r. He closes the door behind him. HOLMES shouts after him.*)

HOLMES. Then bring your cab in here. I want . . .

*   *   *   *   *

(*Over-lap.*)

HOLMES. (*He lapses into a series of groans and remonstrances.*) Why didn't somebody stop him? These cabmen! What did he bring me in here for? It's a conspiracy. I won't stay in this place.

WATSON. Parsons, take that man's number. (*WATSON turns to HOLMES. MADGE opens her handbag and takes out a bottle of smelling salts.*) Now, sir, if you'll sit quiet for one moment, I'll have a look at you! (*WATSON goes s. r. behind the 3-fold screen as MADGE crosses s. l. to HOLMES offering the bottle of smelling salts to HOLMES.*)

*   *   *   *   *

HOLMES. Oh, madam, a friend in need is a friend indeed. (*MADGE realizes something is wrong and turns to the windows s. r. but is blocked by WATSON who comes around the s. r. side of the 3-fold screen. She turns and moves* D. C. *then swings around to run for the double doors up center.*) I wonder pretty lady, would you . . . (HOLMES *jumps up out of his chair and moves* U. C. *to the closed double doors blocking her from opening them to escape. She turns and starts* S. R. *for the windows.*) Don't let her get to that window. (WATSON *blocks her. She stops near the desk and then moves* S. L. *toward the dispensary door.*)

WATSON. Is that *you,* Holmes?

HOLMES. (*He pulls off his glasses and rubber mask.*) Quite so. (HOLMES *crosses* D. S. C. *to the* U. S. *end of the desk where he puts down his disguise on the* U. S. L. *end of the desk.* MADGE *runs* D. S. L. *and exits out through the dispensary door.*)

WATSON. Look out, Holmes! (WATSON *crosses to the dispensary.*) *She can get out that way.*

HOLMES. I don't think so. (HOLMES *opens the cigarette box on the* U. S. R. *end of the desk and takes out a cigarette.*) Ah! I'm glad to see that you keep a few prescriptions carefully done up. Good for the nerves!

FORMAN. (*He comes in through the double doors.*) I've got her, sir!

WATSON. Good heavens! Is that *Forman?* (FORMAN *pulls off his hat and mustache and nods to* WATSON. WATSON *sits in the* D. L. *chair.*)

HOLMES. Has Inspector Bradstreet arrived with his men? (HOLMES *lights his cigarette.*)

FORMAN. Yes, sir. One of em's in the hall there 'olding her. The others are in the kitchen garden. They came in over the back wall from Mortimer Street. (HOLMES *indicates for* FORMAN *to guard the double doors.* FORMAN *moves* U. C. *to the doors, closes them and then stands with his back to the audience.* HOLMES *sits in the chair* S. R. *of the desk.* WATSON *gets up and crosses* S. R. C. *and sits in the chair* S. L. *of the desk.*)

HOLMES. One moment. My dear doctor . . . as you doubtless gather from the little episode that has just taken place, we are making the arrests. The scoundrels are hot on my track. To get me out of the way is the one chance left to them . . . and I'm taking advantage of their pursuit to draw them where we can quietly lay our hand on them . . . one by one. We've made a pretty good haul already . . . four last night in the gas chamber . . . six this afternoon in various places, but I regret to say that up to this time the Professor himself has so far not risen to the bait.

WATSON. Where do you think he is now?

HOLMES. In the open streets, under some clever disguise watching for a chance to get at me.

WATSON. (*He turns in his chair to look* s. L. *in the direction that* MADGE *made her escape.*) And was this woman sent in here to spy . . . (WATSON *turns to* HOLMES.)

HOLMES. Quite so. A spy . . . to let them know by some signal, probably at that window . . .

WATSON. The blinds!

HOLMES. If she found me in the house. And it has just occurred to me that it might not be such a bad idea to try the Professor with *that* bait! Forman!

FORMAN. (*He turns around and moves down to the* U. S. L. *end of the desk.*) Yes, sir!

HOLMES. Bring that Larrabee woman back in here for a moment, and when I light a fresh cigarette, let go your hold on her, carelessly, as if your attention was attracted to something else. Pick her up again when I say.

FORMAN. Very good, sir! Mrs. Larrabee lads, Mr. Holmes would like a word with her. (FORMAN *turns and goes* U. C. *and steps just outside the double doors into the hallway and speaks to the officers outside.* MADGE *enters held by* FORMAN *who keeps a hold onto her left arm as they move* D. S. C.)

HOLMES. Ah, Mrs. Larrabee, I took the liberty of having you brought in for a moment in order to convey to you in a few fitting words my sincere sympathy in your rather unpleasant predicament.

MADGE. It's a lie! A lie! There's no predicament.

HOLMES. Ah, I'm charmed to gather from your rather forcible observation that you do not regard it as such. Quite right, too. Our prisons are so well conducted nowadays. Quite as comfortable as most of the hotels. Quieter and more orderly.

MADGE. How the prisons are conducted is no concern of mine! There is nothing they can hold me for . . . nothing!

HOLMES. (*He stands up and puts out his cigarette in the ashtray.*) There may be something in that. (HOLMES *opens the cigarette box and takes out another cigarette.*) Still, it occurred to me that you might prefer to be near your unfortunate husband, eh? (HOLMES *moves around the* U. S. *end of the desk crossing* C. S. *toward* MADGE *and* FORMAN.) We hear a great deal about the heroic devotion of wives, and all that rubbish. (HOLMES *crosses in front of* MADGE *and* FORMAN. FORMAN *turns to* HOLMES *letting go of* MADGE. *She runs* S. R. *to the windows and pulls up one of the shades.*) You know, Mrs. Larrabee, when we come right down to it, you'd 'ave done a great deal better on your own. (HOLMES *lights his cigarette.*) Many thanks. (*To* FORMAN.) That's all, Forman. Pick her up again. (FORMAN *crosses* S. R. *to* MADGE *and takes hold of her as he moves her to the* U. S. L. *end of the desk and stands behind her holding onto her arm.* HOLMES *sits on the arm of the* D. L. *chair.*) Doctor, would you kindly pull the blind down once more. I don't want you shot from the street. (WATSON *gets up and goes around the* D. S. *side of the desk and pulls the shade down; then he moves to his desk and stands.*)

MADGE. Ah! It's too late.

HOLMES. Too late, eh?

MADGE. The signal is given. You will hear from him soon.

HOLMES. It wouldn't surprise me at all. I expect to hear (*The DOOR BELL RINGS.*) from him *now.* (*Off stage right,* BILLY *is heard shouting, "Sir! Sir!"* BILLY *struggles with* PARSONS *trying to get into* WATSON'S *office. He runs in carrying several newspapers and goes to* HOLMES D. L. C.) Let him go, Parsons. (PARSONS *stands* U. C. *to the left of the double doors.*)

BILLY. He's just come, sir.

HOLMES. From where?

BILLY. The house across the street; he was in there a-watchin' these windows. He must 'ave seen something, for he's just come out . . . there was a cab waitin' in the street for the doctor and he's changed places with the driver.

HOLMES. Where did the driver go?

BILLY. He slunk away in the dark, sir, but he ain't gone far, an' there's two or three more 'angin about.

HOLMES. (*Slight motion of head towards* FORMAN.) Ah, another driver tonight.

BILLY. They're all in it, sir, an' they're a-layin' to get you in that cab w'en you come out, sir! But don't you do it, sir!

HOLMES. Get out again quick, Billy, and keep your eyes peeled!

BILLY. Yes, sir! (BILLY *exits through the double doors and off* U. R. WATSON *is sitting behind his desk.*)

HOLMES. Watson, can you let me have a heavy portmanteau for a few moments?

WATSON. Parsons, go and fetch my large Gladstone . . . bring it here!

PARSONS. Yes, sir. (*He exits off* U. R.)

WATSON. I'm afraid it's a pretty shabby looking . . . (MADGE *tries to break away from* FORMAN'S *grip trying to reach the* S. R. *windows but* FORMAN *holds onto her.* HOLMES *stands up and moves* C. S.)

HOLMES. Many thanks, Mrs. Larrabee, but your *first* signal is all that we require. By it you informed

your friend Moriarty that I was here in the house.
You wish to signal that there is danger. There *is*
danger, Mrs. Larrabee, but I don't care to have you
let him know it. (HOLMES *turns* S. L. *and moves* D. S.
in front of the D. S. L. *chair.*) Take her out, Forman,
and make her comfortable and happy. And by the
way, you might tell the inspector to wait. I could
send him one more. You can't tell! (FORMAN *starts to
move toward the double doors* U. C. *with* MADGE *when
she pulls away from him and moves quickly to* HOLMES
and stops short beside him. She looks at HOLMES, *snaps
her fingers in his face and turns* U. S. C. *laughing as she
exits* U. L. *with* FORMAN. FORMAN *hands her over to a*
POLICE OFFICER *who escorts her off* U. L.) That's a
fine woman! And yet, her crime is commonplace.
(PARSONS *enters carrying a large portmanteau or
Gladstone valise. He places it* C. S. *level with the* U. S. L.
corner of WATSON'S *desk. It is placed so that the straps
of the valise overhang the* D. S. *side. A set of handcuffs are preset between the handles of the valise.
There is a large blue name tag on the* D. S. *handle to
help disguise the handcuffs.*) Put it down there. PAR-
SONS, you ordered a cab for the doctor a short time
ago. It has been waiting, I believe.

PARSONS. Yes, sir, I think it 'as.

HOLMES. Be so good as to tell the driver, the one
you'll now find there, to come in here and get a valise.
Make sure that he comes in himself. When he comes,
tell him that is the one. (PARSONS *exits closing the
double doors behind him and goes off* U. R. HOLMES
crosses to the U. S. *end of* WATSON'S *desk and takes out
a cigarette from the cigarette box.*)

WATSON. But surely he won't come in.

HOLMES. Surely he will! It's his only chance to get
me into that cab! He will take almost any risk for
that. (HOLMES *puts the cigarette into his mouth,
picks up a box of matches from the desk and takes*

out a match.) In times like this . . . (HOLMES *strikes the match and holds it up to the cigarette about to light it.*) you should tell your man never to take the first cab that comes . . . not yet the second . . . the third . . . (HOLMES *lights the cigarette.*)

WATSON. But in this case . . .

HOLMES. In this case I speak for your future guidance. (PARSONS *opens the double doors and is followed by* MORIARTY *disguised as a cab driver.* MORIARTY *moves* D. S. *to the portmanteau.*)

PARSONS. 'Ere it is. Right in, this way. (HOLMES *shakes* WATSON'S *hand and picks up some loose papers on* WATSON'S *desk. As he turns to* MORIARTY, *he slips the papers into his left side coat pocket. He still has the cigarette in his mouth.*)

HOLMES. Well, goodbye, old fellow! I'll write you from Paris. Be so good as to keep me fully informed as to the progress of events. (PARSONS *closes the double doors as he exits* U. R. MORIARTY *kneels by the valise checking the straps.* HOLMES *moves* S. L. C. *then turns* U. S. *and kneels facing* MORIARTY *on the other side of the valise.* HOLMES *puts the handcuffs onto* MORIARTY.) As for these papers, I'll attend to them personally. Here, my man, help me to tighten these straps, will you. There are a few little things in this bag that I wouldn't like to lose, eh. You never can tell the railways are so unreliable these days. (HOLMES *snaps shut the handcuffs onto* MORIARTY. HOLMES *stands up as he takes hold of the* S. L. *side of* MORIARTY'S *scarf and moves* S. R. *around the* U. S. R. *side of the valise removing the scarf and* MORIARTY'S *hat as he moves* S. L. *dropping the scarf and hat into the examining chair.* HOLMES *then moves* D. L. *near the* D. L. *chair and the dispensary. He is still smoking the cigarette in his mouth.* MORIARTY *rises slowly then quickly brings his arms up showing that he's been handcuffed.*) Doctor, be so good as to strike the bell two or three times in

rapid succession. (WATSON *taps the bell on his desk.*
HOLMES *sits in the* D. L. *chair as* FORMAN *enters and
moves down to the* S. R. *side of* MORIARTY.) Forman!
    FORMAN. Yes, sir.
    HOLMES. Got a man there with you?
    FORMAN. Yes, sir, the Inspector came in himself,
sir.
    HOLMES. Ah, the Inspector himself. We shall read
graphic accounts in tomorrow morning's paper of the
difficult and dangerous arrest he succeeded in making
at Doctor Watson's house in Kensington. Take him
out, Forman, and introduce them. They'll be charmed
to meet. (FORMAN *takes hold of* MORIARTY *but* MORI-
ARTY *pullls away from him and looks at* HOLMES.)
Wait! See what he wants! (FORMAN *goes* U. C. *and
stands outside the double doors leaving the double
doors opened and he faces front.* WATSON *sits at his
desk and carefully opens the top,* D. S. *drawer, and
puts his hand on a revolver. It is a move that is
hardly noticed.*)
    MORIARTY. Do you imagine, Sherlock Holmes, *that
this is the end?*
    HOLMES. I ventured to dream that it might be.
    MORIARTY. Are you quite sure the police will be able
to hold me?
    HOLMES. I am quite sure of nothing.
    MORIARTY. Ah! I have heard that you are planning
to take a little trip . . . you and your friend here
. . . a little trip on the Continent.
    HOLMES. And if I do?
    MORIARTY. I shall meet you there. You will change
your course . . . you will try to elude me . . . but
whichever way you turn, there will be eyes that see and
wires that tell. I shall meet you there . . . and you
know it. And when I fall, you will fall with me.
(MORIARTY *backs* U. C. *and out between the double
doors where he pauses looking at* HOLMES *before exiting with* FORMAN *and* TWO POLICEMEN *off* U. R.)

WATSON. *We could give up the trip Holmes!*

HOLMES. (*He slouches down in his chair holding his cigarette in his left hand.*) Was ever such a dreary, dismal, unprofitable world?

WATSON. My dear Holmes, don't be downcast! Your most ruthless adversary is behind bars.

HOLMES. Psshaw, my dear Doctor. (HOLMES *stands and moves* C. S.) Then my own little practice will degenerate into an agency for the recovering of lost lead pencils . . . (HOLMES *moves* S. R. *to the chair* S. L. *of the desk.*) and giving advice to young ladies from boarding schools. Crime is commonplace, existence is commonplace, no qualities save the commonplace have any future on this earth. (HOLMES *sits in the chair.*) But he'll get out. But I mustn't indulge my mordid fantasies now. The worst is yet to come. (WATSON *stands and looks at his pocket watch then moves around the* U. S. *side of his desk and goes to the* S. L. *side of* HOLMES.)

WATSON. Why, good heavens, Holmes! We've barely five minutes to get to Baker Street. Your appointment with Sir Edward and the Count to receive that package of letters.

HOLMES. No, it is alright. They are coming here. (HOLMES *takes out the papers he had stuffed into his left inside coat pocket when* MORIARTY *had entered and drops them onto the* U. S. *end of* WATSON's *desk.*)

WATSON. Here?

HOLMES. That is, if you will be so good as to permit it. (WATSON *goes to the* U. S. *side of the portmanteau and carries it to the* S. L. *side of the dispensary wall where he puts it down. He then moves* D. S. *and stands in front of the* D. L. *chair.*)

WATSON. Certainly. But why not at Baker Street?

HOLMES. The police wouldn't allow us through the ropes.

WATSON. Police! Ropes!

HOLMES. Police . . . ropes . . . ladders . . . hose . . . crowds . . . fire engines . . .

WATSON. Why, you don't mean that . . .

HOLMES. Quite so, the villains have burned me out.

WATSON. Good heavens . . . burned you . . . oh, that's too bad. (WATSON *sits in the* D. L. *chair.*) What did you lose?

HOLMES. Everything! I'm so glad of it! This one thing that I shall do . . . here, in a few moments . . . is the end.

WATSON. You mean . . . Miss Faulkner? (HOLMES *turns to* WATSON.)

HOLMES. Watson . . . there were four to one against me! They said, *"Come here,"* I said, *"Stay close to me,"* and she did! She clung to me. I could feel her heart beating against mine. She trusted me . . . and I was playing a game! It is a dangerous game . . . but I do play it! It will be the same tonight! She'll be there . . . I'll be here! She'll listen . . . she'll believe . . . and she'll trust me . . . and I'll be playing the game . . . *NO MORE* . . . I've had enough! It's my last case. Oh well! What does it matter? Life is a brief affair at best. A few sunrises and sunsets. The warm breath of a few summers. The cold chill of a few winters . . . and then . . . (HOLMES *pauses.*)

WATSON. And then . . . ? (HOLMES *turns* S. R. *and picks up a large book on the* D. S. R. *end of* WATSON'S *desk.*)

HOLMES. And then. (*He begins to look through the book.*)

WATSON. My dear Holmes, I'm afraid that plan of gaining her confidence and regard went a little further than you intended.

HOLMES. A trifle!

WATSON. For her . . . or for you?

HOLMES. For her . . . and for me.

WATSON. But, if you both love each other . . .

HOLMES. (*He snaps the book shut and stands mov-*

ing to C. S. *with the book.*) Love! Who spoke that word? Love is an emotional thing and is therefore opposed to the true, cold reason which I place above all things. I should never marry myself, lest I bias my judgment. Women are never to be trusted entirely, not the best of them. I assure you the most winning woman I ever knew was hanged for poisoning her three little children for the insurance money. No, no. (HOLMES *goes* D. L. *to the dispensary door and places the book on the floor so that the dispensary door will stay ajar once* ALICE *goes into the dispensary.*) I must cure Miss Faulkner of her regard for me while there's time. She's coming here. (WATSON *stands and moves* C. S. *then turns* S. L. *to* HOLMES.)

WATSON. She won't come alone?

HOLMES. No, Terese will be with her. When she comes, let her wait in that room. You can manage that.

WATSON. Certainly! (*The DOOR BELL RINGS.*)

HOLMES. She may be there now. Can I go to your dressing room, and brush away some of this dust.

WATSON. (*He moves to the* U. S. L. *end of his desk.*) By all means! (WATSON *turns* S. L. *to* HOLMES *who has moved* C. S. WATSON *moves toward him.*) My wife is in the drawing-room. Do look in on her a moment. It will please her so much.

HOLMES. It will more than please me! (HOLMES *goes* U. C. *and opens the double doors. A piano is heard playing softly in the background.* HOLMES *turns quickly and moves* D. S. C.) Home! Love! Life! (HOLMES *looks at* WATSON.) Ah, Watson!

(HOLMES *turns quickly* U. S. *and exits through the double doors closing them behind him. He goes upstairs. The piano music stops when the double doors are closed.* WATSON *stands behind his desk and picks up a photo that is on the* U. S. *section of his desk. He looks at it a moment then puts it*

on the D. S. *end of the desk and sits.* PARSONS
*enters. The piano music is heard faintly in the
background while the doors are opened.*)

PARSONS. Excuse me, sir. A young lady, sir, wants
to speak to you. If there's anyone 'ere, she won't come
in.

WATSON. Any name?

PARSONS. No, sir. I asked and she said it was unnecessary as you wouldn't know 'er. She 'as 'er maid
with 'er, sir.

WATSON. Then it must be. Show her in. (PARSONS
starts to exit when WATSON *stops him.* WATSON *stands
up and moves toward* PARSONS.) And, Parsons, two
gentlemen, Count von Stalburg and Sir Edward Leighton will call. Bring them here and then tell Mr.
Holmes. You'll find him in my dressing room.

PARSONS. Yes, sir.

WATSON. Send everybody else away. I'll see that
lady now.

PARSONS. Yes, sir. (PARSONS *exits closing the doors
behind him and he goes off* U. R. *then he re-appears
and opens the doors for* ALICE FAULKNER *to enter. She
moves* D. C. *The piano music in the background stops
as* PARSONS *closes the double doors and exits* U. R.)

ALICE. Is this . . . is this Doctor Watson's room?

WATSON. Yes, and I am Doctor Watson. (WATSON
moves toward her.)

ALICE. Is . . . would you mind telling me if Mr.
Holmes . . . Mr. Sherlock Holmes is here?

WATSON. He will be before long, Miss . . . er . . .

ALICE. My name is Faulkner.

WATSON. Miss Faulkner. He arrived a short while
ago, but has gone upstairs for a few moments.

ALICE. Oh! And is he coming down soon?

WATSON. Well, the fact is, Miss Faulkner, he has an
appointment with two gentlemen here, and I was to
let him know as soon as they arrived.

ALICE. Do you suppose I could wait without troubling you to much and see him *afterwards?*

WATSON. Why, certainly.

ALICE. Thank you, and I . . . I don't want· him to know that I . . . that I came.

WATSON. Of course, if you wish, there's no need of my telling him.

ALICE. It's very important *indeed* that you *don't,* Doctor Watson. I can explain it all to you afterwards.

WATSON. No explanation is necessary, Miss Faulkner.

ALICE. Thank you. I suppose there is a waiting room for patients? (WATSON *crosses* s. l. *to the dispensary and shifts the* D. L. *chair further* D. S. *as he moves to the dispensary door.*)

WATSON. Yes, or you could sit over there in my dispensary. You'll be less likely to be disturbed.

ALICE. Yes, thank you. I think I would rather be where it's entirely quiet. (*DOOR BELL RINGS. She crosses* s. l. *to the dispensary door which* WATSON *has pushed open for her.*)

WATSON. Then step this way. I think the gentlemen have arrived. (*He crosses below the* D. L. *chair and moves* U. C. ALICE *turns to him.*)

ALICE. And when the business between the gentlemen is over, could you please have some one tell me?

WATSON. I'll tell you myself, Miss Faulkner.

ALICE. Thank you. (*She goes into the dipensary and sits down. The dispensary door is slightly ajar because of the book* HOLMES *has put on the floor to keep the door from closing.* PARSONS *enters and stands to the left of the double doors as* COUNT VON STALBURG *and* SIR EDWARD LEIGHTON *enter and stand to the right of the double doors.*)

PARSONS. Count von Stalburg and Sir Edward Leighton. (PARSONS *takes their top hats from them and exits closing the doors after him and exiting* U. R.)

WATSON. Count . . . Sir Edward.

Sir Edward. Dr. Watson. Good evening. Our appointment with Mr. Holmes was changed to your house, I believe.

Watson. Quite right, Sir Edward. (Watson *crosses to the* s. r. *to move the chair* s. l. *of the desk to* s. l. c. *near the* d. l. *chair for* Sir Edward *and the* Count.) Pray be seated, gentlemen. (Sir Edward *and the* Count *cross* d. l. *and the* Count *sits in the* d. l. *chair and* Sir Edward *sits in the chair just* u. s. *of him.* Watson *crosses* s. r. *below his desk and sits behind his desk.*)

von Stalburg. Mr. Holmes is a trifle late.

Watson. He has already arrived, Count. I have sent for him.

von Stalburg. Ugh!

Sir. Edward. It was quite a surprise to receive his message an hour ago changing the place of meeting. We should otherwise have gone to his house in Baker Street.

Watson. You would have found it in ashes, Sir Edward.

Sir Edward. What! Really!

von Stalburg. Ugh!

Sir Edward. The . . . the house burnt!

Watson. Burning now, probably.

Sir Edward. I'm very sorry to hear this. It must be a severe blow to him.

Watson. No, he minds it very little.

Sir Edward. Really! I should hardly have thought it.

von Stalburg. Do I understand you to say, doctor, that you have sent for Mr. Holmes?

Watson. Yes, Count, and he'll be coming shortly. (Watson *stands and moves around to the* u. s. l. *end of his desk.*) Indeed, I think I hear his step upon the stairs now. (Holmes *opens the double doors and enters closing the doors behind him.* Sir Edward *and the* Count *stand.*)

HOLMES. Gentlemen, be seated again, I beg. (WATSON
moves back to his desk chair and sits. SIR EDWARD
and the COUNT *take their seats as* HOLMES *moves*
D. R. C. *near* WATSON'S *desk.*) Our busines tonight can
be very quickly disposed of. You were not.fied to come
here this evening in order that I might deliver into
your hands the package which you engaged me, on
behalf of your exalted client, to recover. I must say,
in justice to myself, that but for that agreement on
my part and the consequent steps which you took
upon the basis of it, I would never have continued
with the work. As it was, however, I felt bound to do
so and therefore pursued the matter to the very end
and I now have the honor to deliver it. (HOLMES *takes*
the package out from his left hand inside coat pocket
and puts it on the D. S. L. *end of* WATSON'S *desk. He*
moves C. S. *facing* SIR EDWARD *who stands as the*
COUNT *stands and goes* S. R. *to pick up the package.*
The COUNT *tears open the package to examine the*
contents.)

SIR EDWARD. Permit me to congratulate you, Mr.
Holmes, upon the marvelous skill you have displayed,
and the promptness with which you have fulfilled
your agreement. (HOLMES *moves* U. C.)

VON STALBURG. Oh! No! No! No! (SIR EDWARD *moves*
S. R. *to the* COUNT. *The* COUNT *hands* SIR EDWARD *the*
jewel case and photographs but hold onto the letters.)

SIR EDWARD. What does this mean?

VON STALBURG. These letters!!!

SIR EDWARD. And these other things. Where did you
get them?

HOLMES. I purchased them last night.

SIR EDWARD. Purchased them?

HOLMES. Quite so.

VON STALBURG. From whom, if I may ask?

HOLMES. From whom? From the parties concerned
. . . by consent of Miss Faulkner.

VON STALBURG. You have been deceived.

HOLMES. What! (HOLMES *goes to* VON STALBURG *and grabs some of the letters out of his hand.* HOLMES *crosses* D. S. L. *removing one of the letters from its envelop then reaches into the left side of his pocket and takes out a magnifying glass and holds it up to examine the letter.*).

VON STALBURG. This package contains nothing . . . not a single letter or paper that we wanted. (*He moves* C. S. *toward* HOLMES.) All clever imitations! The photographs are of another person! You have been duped. In spite of your supposed cleverness they have tricked you!

SIR EDWARD. Most decidedly duped, Mr. Holmes! Oh, dear Lord, what will the minister say.

HOLMES. Why, this is terrible!

SIR EDWARD. Terrible! Surely, sir, you do not mean by that, that there is a possibility you may not be able to recover them!

HOLMES. That is quite true! (WATSON *gets up and moves* D. R. *just off the platform unit and the* COUNT *moves* S. R. *above the desk.*)

SIR EDWARD. After your positive assurance! After the steps we have taken in the matter by your advice!

VON STALBURG. Surely, sir, you don't mean there is no hope of it? (*He sits in* WATSON's *chair behind the desk.*)

HOLMES. I'm afraid that there is none whatever, Count. (*He sits in the* D. L. *chair.*)

SIR EDWARD. Why, this is scandalous! It is criminal, sir! Have you any idea what this will mean in terms of diplomatic consequences for Her Majesty's government. You had no right to mislead us in this way, and you shall certainly suffer the consequences. I shall see that you are brought into court to answer for it, Mr. Holmes. It will be such a blow to your reputation that you . . .

HOLMES. (*He gets up and moves* D. S. L.) There is nothing to do, Sir Edward. I am ruined . . . ruined

. . . (ALICE *appears in the dispensary doorway holding the package in her right hand.*)

ALICE. He is not ruined, Sir Edward. (*She crosses c. s. to* SIR EDWARD. HOLMES *turns to watch her as she is about to hand the package to* SIR EDWARD. *She stops and turns to* HOLMES; *then goes to* HOLMES *and gives the package to him.* HOLMES *takes it, crosses c. s. to* SIR EDWARD *and takes out his pocket watch.*)

HOLMES. Gentlemen, I notified you in my letter of this morning that the package should be produced at a quarter past nine. It is fourteen and one half minutes past. (HOLMES *puts his pocket watch away.*)

SIR EDWARD and VON STALBURG. Ah! Excellent! Admirable, Mr. Holmes! It is all clear now! Really marvellous! Yes, upon my word! (*The* COUNT *and* SIR EDWARD *stop muttering when* HOLMES *runs to* ALICE *and gives the package back to her.*)

HOLMES. Take this. It is yours. Never give it up. Use it only for what you wish!

SIR EDWARD. What! We are not to have it.

HOLMES. You are not to have it.

SIR EDWARD. After all this?

HOLMES. After all this.

*   *   *   *   *

(*Over-lap.*)

VON STALBURG. But, my dear sir . . .

SIR EDWARD. This is outrageous! Your agreement?

*   *   *   *   *

HOLMES. I break it! Do what you please. Warrants . . . summons . . . arrests . . . will find me here. Watson, get them out! Get them away!

WATSON. (*He crosses u. c. to open the double doors.*) I'm sure, gentlemen, that you will appreciate the considerable strain under which Mr. Holmes has been working. (ALICE *crosses* S. C. *to* SIR EDWARD *and the* COUNT *holding out the package to* SIR EDWARD.)

ALICE. Wait a moment, Doctor Watson! Here is the package, Sir Edward! (*She is just about to give it to* SIR EDWARD *who reaches for it.*)

HOLMES. No! (ALICE *stops and looks at* HOLMES. SIR EDWARD *still has his hand out for the package almost touching it.*)

ALICE. Yes. I much prefer that he should have them. Since you came to me that night and asked me to give them to you, I have thought of what you said. You were right. It was revenge. (ALICE *hands the package to* SIR EDWARD.)

SIR EDWARD. We are greatly indebted to you, Miss Faulkner. (SIR EDWARD *hands the package to the* COUNT. *The* COUNT *tears open the package and examines it and is satisfied.*)

VON STALBURG. To be sure! To be sure!

SIR EDWARD. And to you, too, Mr. Holmes, if this was a part of the game. It was certainly an extraordinary method of obtaining possession of valuable papers . . . but we won't quarrel with the method as long as it accomplished the desired result! Eh, Count?

VON STALBURG. Certainly not, Sir Edward.

SIR EDWARD. You have only to notify me of the charge for your services, Mr. Holmes, and you will receive a check. I have the honor to wish you good night, Miss Faulkner. Doctor Watson. This way Count. (*The* COUNT *clicks his heels on "good night," on "Miss Faulkner" and clicks twice on "Doctor Watson." They exit* U. C. *followed by* DOCTOR WATSON *who takes a last look at* HOLMES *and* ALICE *before closing the double doors and exiting* U. R. ALICE *goes to the* D. S. R. *corner of* WATSON'S *desk with her back to* HOLMES.)

HOLMES. Now that you think it over, Miss Faulkner, you are doubtless beginning to realize the series of tricks by which I sought to deprive you of your

property. I could not take it out of the house that
night because of course it could have been recovered
by law. I therefore resorted to a cruel and cowardly
device to induce you to relinquish it. (ALICE *turns to
him.*)

ALICE. But you . . . you did not give it to them . . .

HOLMES. No, it was necessary that you should do as
you did.

ALICE. What?

HOLMES. It was a trick . . . to the very end.
(HOLMES *crosses to the* U. S. L. *end of the desk. He
picks up the photographs on the desk and starts to
look at them.* ALICE *still stands at the* D. S. L. *end of
the desk.*) Your maid is waiting. (ALICE *starts to exit*
U. C. *but turns back to* HOLMES.)

ALICE. And was it a trick last night when they tried
to kill you?

HOLMES. I went there to purchase the counterfeit
package to use as you have seen.

ALICE. And did you know that I would come?

HOLMES. No. But it fell in with my plans notwith-
standing. Now that you see me in my true light, Miss
Faulkner, we have nothing left to say but good night
. . . and goodbye . . . which you ought to be very
glad to do. Believe me, I meant no harm to you . . .
it was purely business. For that you see I would
sacrifice everything. Even my supposed friendship for
you was a . . . was a . . . pretense . . . a sham . . .

ALICE. I don't believe you. (HOLMES *throws the
photographs down onto the desk and turns to face
her.*)

HOLMES. Why not?

ALICE. From the way you speak . . . from the way
you look . . . from all sorts of things! You're not the
only one who can tell things from small details.

HOLMES. Your powers of observation are somewhat
remarkable, Miss Faulkner . . . and your deduction
is quite correct! I suppose . . . indeed I know . . .

that I love you. (HOLMES *sits on edge of desk.*) I love you. (ALICE *starts to move toward* HOLMES *but he stops her.*) But, I know as well what I am . . . and what you are . . . I know that no such person as I seared . . . (ALICE *turns away from him opening her hand bag to take out the famous "Sherlock Holmes" meershaum pipe to give him as a present.*) drugged, poisoned, should ever dream of being a part of your sweet life. There is every reason why I should say good-bye and farewell! (ALICE *turns to him offering him the pipe.*) There is every reason . . . (HOLMES *takes the pipe, looks at it in ecstasy, then grabs* ALICE *and kisses her on the mouth.*)

BLACKOUT and CURTAIN

PROPERTY LIST

ACT ONE

Scene 1: *Larrabee Set*
Furniture:
  pink carpet
  hat-stand
  small table
  armchair with false seat
  drum table
  round seat plus 2 cushions in center (round cushion—piano
    stool)
  desk with safe and curtain
  U/R chair
  Grand piano plus stool
  bell-pull
Hand Properties:
On Stage—
  armchair—dummy packet of letters sewn into seat
  drum table—lamp, 5 magazines, paper knife; dressing in
    drawers at 3, 6, and 9 o'clock
  piano—albums 1, 2 and 3 on music rack; pile of music plus
    3 books on folded back lid; framed photograph. OP
    of music rack, silver ashtray and matches (2 heads set
    out) and lamp on body of piano
  desk—dressing inside top for Madge to disarrange; loaded
    club in top left hand drawer and dressing; safe empty,
    catch closed and curtain closed over door; check hole
    started in metal plate of safe door for drilling; 5 framed
    photographs on top of desk
  small table—round silver tray
  upstairs hallway—salver and note and visiting card
  rostrum under stairs—bulldog revolver
Off Stage—
OP Side:
  bundle of evening papers
  1 folded paper
  door bell and door slam FX

Prompt Side—
  U/R piano
  lamp crash FX, stage weight wrapped in hessian for 3
      knocks FX
  sack and baby in shawl, gin bottle and water—for s. c. LINK
  large white jug

SCENE 2: *Moriarty Set*
Furniture:
  desk and chair
Properties and Dressing:
Desk—
  lever box (Fixed down) levers (See sketch)
  blotter and three sheets of paper—top one with corner turned
      down
  silver desk set and one pencil
  telephone—receiver set for R/H
  in-tray plus papers and ledger
  brass bowl and half inch of water
  match-stand and matches—clean striker, one match set out
  speaking-tube—check whistle not jammed in tube
  second telephone (receiver only) on hook on wall PS of
      security door
  "Mona Lisa" and gas mantle on hingeing wall
  2 maps on wall behind chair
  lift in down position
FX—Off Stage behind security door:
  telephone bell
  buzzer

SCENE 3: *Holmes Set*
Furniture:
  red carpet
  armchair, cushion, footstool
  3 large cushions
  bookcase
  sideboard
  table and cloth
  3 U/R chairs
  box fender
  black box

Properties and Dressing:

Laboratory Shelves:

microscope, tray plus "experiment" plus 1 phial (from syringe case) set in oblong dish; also scientific dressing pre-set

Mantlepiece:

clock, curved pipe, 3 boxes of matches (2 heads set out on each box, all boxes "clean"), slipper plus tobacco, syringe case plus syringe plus 2 needles plus 2 phials with corks (the third on the Lab. shelf)

dressing on mantlepiece fixed down, pipe-rack plus 7 pipes, large cherry wood pipe, jar of spills, medicine bottle, tobacco jar, pile of correspondence pinned with knife, letter rack plus papers etc. plus large knife

Table:

cloth plus 4 books (top one—"Psalms"—open), lamp, ash-tray, bell

Sideboard:

decanter of wine. plus glass, lamp, plus other dressing ie. tantalus of 3 decanters, 4 bottles of wine, casket, cigarette box, silver dish, dish lid, bust of Wagner, brandy and wine glasses

Sideboard Drawer:

2 revolvers and box of cartridges in L/H compartment

cutlery pre-set in R/H compartment

Bookcase:

dressing pre-set in cupboard; check cupboard is firmly locked

books fixed to shelves

Coal Scuttle:

set on floor in front of bookcase, lid open, box plus mild cigars in it

Fire-irons:

wired to wall PS end of mantlepiece

check green baize door is un-locked and the key is in the lock

Holmes' black coat (delivered during Scene change by Dresser) on newel post outside green baize door

Off Stage—Prompt Side:

envelope and letter for Billy

electric doorbell FX

ACT TWO

SCENE 1: *Gas Chamber Set*
Furniture:
  table
  2 bentwood chairs
  box ??? in cupboard
  open crate plus dressing (old rope)
  2 closed crates
  small open crate (light leaks sealed)
Properties:
  short pipe plus wooden pulley block in large open crate
  2 pieces of cotton rope coiled together on floor in front of
     open crate
  "Unbreakable" lamp, offstage in hallway upstairs
  safety lamp on Bentwood chair on table
Off Promp Side:
  pram plus dressing for Scene Link plus baby
Off OP:
  barrel organ for Scene Link
  bolt FX—USOP
  whistle FX—USOP
Note—Check slit in door for clasp knife

SCENE 2: *Watson Set*
  desk
  swivel chair (cushion attached)
  U/R chair
  screen
  small table (from Scene 1)
  armchair
  dentist's chair
  instrument table
  U/R chair in Dispensary
  yellow carpet
Properties and Dressing:
On Stage—Desk:
  blotter plus headed note-paper, open diary, ink-stand plus
     in and pen, framed photograph, small book and large
     book, push-bell, cigarette box and cigarettes, silver
     match-box holder and matches, brass ashtray

Screen:
towel

Instrument Table:
white cloth, beaker and cotton wool, steriliser and mirror, tongue spatula, box and "spectacle" reflecting mirror, white napkin, wooden box and bottles, case and bottles

Dispensary:
bottle of medicine on shelf and dressing (see diagram)
certificate and lamp bracket on Prompt Side wall above chair
2 anatomical pictures and lamp bracket on Prompt Side wall of set US of Dispensary

Off Stage: OP—
bundle of papers (reset from Scene 1), large valise and handcuffs, door-slam FX, door-bell FX, cab crash FX—orange box, pipe

Consumable Items:
matches—about 3 "clean" boxes needed per show
cigars—petit corona size for Larrabee's case—3 smoked per show, the 2 spares sometimes broken in Gas Chamber Scene
mild "Embassy," "Hamlet" or similar for box in coal scuttle —1 smoked per show
cigarettes—untipped for Prince. (Player's)
untipped Turkish (Sullivan Powell, Ovals, Sobranie or anything mild) for cigarette box on Watson's desk, 2 per show
tobacco—Erinmore smoking mixture, if unavailable, anything mild
batteries—for safety lamp, replaced about every 2 shows (LX to provide) for cigar torch, replaced only occasionally (LX to provide) also carry spare torch
carry spares for currency notes for Potentate (Joe Charles), visiting cards, newspapers, £100 notes

OFF STAGE SETTINGS

Stage Right:
bundle of evening papers
folded paper
3 large cushions
3 U/R chairs

armchair and red cushion
footstool
laboratory stool
box fender
2 pair of curtains
red carpet
sideboard with fixed cutlery in right hand compartment of
    drawer and two revolvers in left hand compartment of
    drawer and two boxes of cartridges
coal scuttle and coal
fire-irons
bookcase—cupboard dressed, book fixed on shelves
black box
large valise and hand-cuffs
4 large books
folding coat rack
table and cloth
barrell organ
clock
tray and fixed chemical glass
empty tray for Scene 1 props

Tray with Scene 3 Properties:
    box with cigars, slipper with tobacco, large ash tray, red
        curved pipe, hand-bell, hypodermic box with syringe,
        2 needles, 3 bottles, 3 boxes of matches (all clean, each
        set with two matches), Larrabee letter and envelope,
        key for green door

Tray with Properties for Side-board:
    4 bottles of wine (Madeira, Chateau Latour, Port, Puligny-
        Montrachet), 7 wine glasses, decanter bottle with brandy,
        dish and cover, Wagner bust, casket, wooden inlaid
        cigar box, tantalus with three bottles and contents

Sound Effects Live:
    bolt board and short pipe
    door-slam
    hand-bell for door-bell
    apple crate and pipe (used for sound effects in cab crash)

Stage Left:
    upright piano
    mantlepiece and fixed dressing
    curtain to mask security door for Act Two
    plain wooden table

2 Bentwood chairs
1 large open crate and dressing (old rope) and short pipe and
    pulley-block
2 large closed crates
small open box
desk and Scene 5 props packed in drawers
yellow carpet
framed certificate and 2 anatomical pictures
upright chair for dispensary
swivel chair with cushion attached and upright chair for desk
armchair
screen and towel
dentist's chair
narrow black table
dressing fixed on dispensary shelves
pram and dressing
Property Table:
  baby and shawl
  small bottle with water
  cotton rope
  brown bottle of medicine
  whistle for F/X
  sack filled with rags
Sound Effects—Live:
  (For lamp crash) Carton, glass, hammer, weight
  stage weight wrapped in hessian (For thuds)
  electric bell (Door bell, Scene 3)

COSTUME PLOT

SHERLOCK HOLMES:
 ebony cane, card case with personal calling cards, small notebook with diary pencil, pocket watch on a chain, six .38 calibre bullets, straight pipe, violin case with violin and two bows inside (one bow is soaped to make no sound when rubbed across the strings; the other bow is rosined), a bundle of 100 pound notes (the top 10 notes are loose; the bottom 10 notes are taped together) with a band around them, a dummy flashlight cigar size to be used as a spare in the GAS CHAMBER in case the real cigar should not work, a magnifying glass with a handle and one pair of pince-nez

MORIARTY:
 pocket watch on a chain, a cane, one large revolver and a memorandum notebook

JAMES LARRABEE:
 a leather cigar case holding three to five cigars, a box of matches, a pocket watch on a chain with a silver whistle attached, a dummy package of jewelry, letters and photographs which can have a small red tag on it to help distinguish it from the genuine package

SIDNEY PRINCE:
 a leather satchel to carry his tools which are wrapped in a cloth, rolled up and tied; a stethoscope which is in the leather satchel, a pocket sized notebook and pencil, a gold cigarette case with at least three cigarettes in it, a box of matches, a pocket watch on a chain with a whistle attached

DOCTOR WATSON:
 a flower for his buttonhole for the Baker Street Scene, a gold watch on a chain, a box of matches and two bottles of medicine (one green and one brown)

FORMAN:
 a Sherlock Holmes calling card, two coins, a handkerchief, a coach whip and spectacles which are used as part of his disguise with Holmes in Doctor Watson's Office

MADGE LARRABEE:

handkerchief, a knitting bag, two coins, an evening bag with a handkerchief in it and smelling salts

ALICE FAULKNER:

the real package of jewelry, letters and photographs which can have a yellow tag on it to help distinguish it from the dummy. A Sherlock Holmes calling card, a handbag with a Calabash pipe in it, earrings and a brooch

BASSICK:

pocket size notebook and pencil, a silver watch on a chain, spectacles and a truncheon

CRAIGIN:

a jack-knife and a brownish, soft cotton rope used to tie up Alice Faulkner

LIGHTFOOT McTAGUE:

a handkerchief which is used as a gag for Alice Faulkner, a jack-knife and a piece of heavy rope that is wound around in several loops

THOMAS LEARY:

a Victorian magazine, i.e., comic book style, and a stump of a pencil

COUNT VON STALBURG:

a silver watch on a chain with a jewelled charm; a monocle

SIR EDWARD LEIGHTON:

a silver watch on a chain with a fob seal

OLD LADY:

two coins

NEWSBOY:

several newspapers folded

VIOLINIST:

tin cup with a string that hangs on his violin

INDIAN PRINCE:

ivory topped cane and a bundle of paper currency

REAL ESTATE MAN:

pocket size notebook and pencil and several coins

PENNY WHISTLER:

penny whistle and several coins

OLD CHINAMAN:

folded paper used for dope

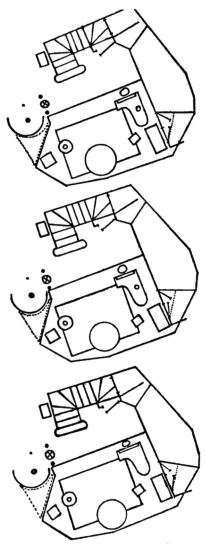

ACT ONE
Scene One
LARRABEE'S

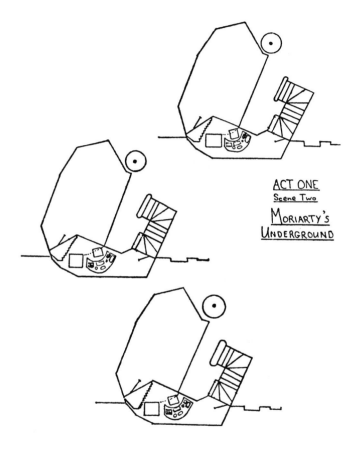

ACT ONE
Scene Two

MORIARTY'S
UNDERGROUND

141

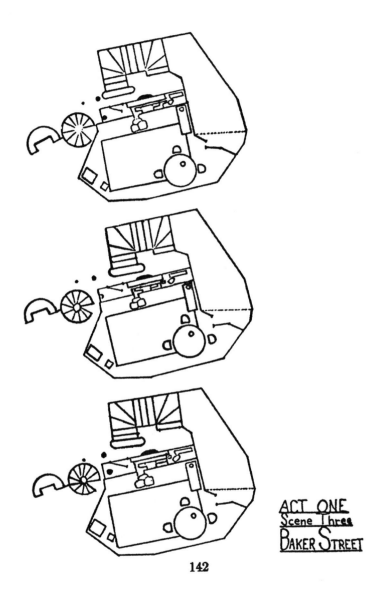

ACT ONE
Scene Three
BAKER STREET

142

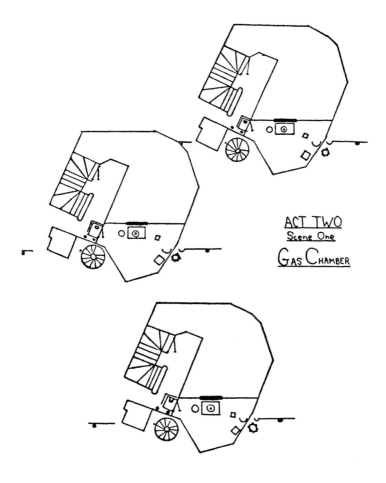

ACT TWO
Scene One

GAS CHAMBER

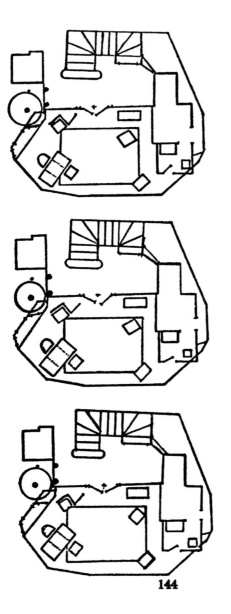

ACT TWO
Scene Three
DOCTOR WATSON

144

CPSIA information can be obtained at www.ICGtesting.com
Printed in the USA
BVOW031330041211

277440BV00004B/5/P